The of Cromwell's Skull

C000121204

A Gentleman Detective Mystery

Evelyn James

Red Raven Publications 2023

www.sophie-jackson.com

Contents

Chapter One

C olonel Bainbridge was sitting in his private study quietly musing over a small selection of papers. They were all the documents he had so far gathered in relation to the murder of his business partner, friend and fellow detective, Houston Fairchild.

Houston's murder, and the bank robbery that had pre-empted it, remained unsolved, and Bainbridge feared that would always be the case. He had never supposed the one case that would haunt him for the rest of his days because he could not crack it, would be the one involving his dearest friend.

Bainbridge would come to his study and look at the papers whenever his thoughts turned to Houston. At one time that had been daily, now the pain and regret had softened, and these glum musings came over him less frequently. It was over a month since he had last pulled out the papers.

He knew the contents of them all by heart, though he still liked to look at them, and go through his notes to refresh his memory. He studied the papers for a while longer, then put them aside.

Nothing new was springing to mind.

Bainbridge raised his head to look at a photograph hanging on the wall above his desk. It was a sepia coloured image, a reprint from a photograph taken by the local newspaper just a short time before Houston died. Bainbridge and Houston were standing outside a building with another man, who was pretending to thank them for their help while smiling at the camera. Bainbridge looked serious, his belly thrust out, his moustache masking any expression on his mouth.

Houston was smiling a broad, childish grin of delight at the attention. Houston was the handsome one in the partnership. He was slender, without being effete, rugged without being weathered, and could charm, as he liked to put it, the rattle out of a rattlesnake.

Houston was American, and he attracted the ladies because of his intriguing accent and mysterious past with the Pinkerton Agency. He could have had any woman he liked, had he wished.

Bainbridge smiled at the picture; chalk and cheese they had been, and it had worked well. Now here he was, working with his niece, Victoria Bovington. She was nothing like Bainbridge, but she was also nothing like Houston. She was her own person, with her own mind, which was rather radical for a woman in that day and age. Bainbridge secretly approved.

He was just thinking how strangely life wove around you and caught you out, when there was knock at his study door. He knew Victoria's knock when he heard it, he also knew how taxing she found it to restrain herself from immediately entering the room. His gentle attempts to have her respect his privacy had so far had limited effect; the only rooms he had convinced her she should not enter without permission were his bedroom and this study. The former he had achieved largely because she had walked in on him once in his pyjamas, the latter he managed by locking his study door.

Victoria was the sort of person who was always rushing from place to place, and found asking permission to enter rooms an infuriating waste of time.

"You can enter, it is not locked," Bainbridge called out, deciding not to try her patience for too long.

At least he knew Victoria only bothered him in his study when it was important, not like Mrs Huggins, his housekeeper, who would pester him over all manner of mundane matters.

Victoria entered the room and glanced warily at his desk. She knew he tended to come up here to mull over Houston. She was pleased to see there were no papers before him.

Victoria was a fashionable young lady who, at first glance, would appear more interested in evening soirees, and the theatre than the rough and tumble of detective work. Few who came to this initial conclusion remained misguided for long, at least not once they had spent some time in Victoria's company.

While some aspects of detective work had not come naturally to her, she had learned to master all that was required, and she was certainly nobody's fool. Bainbridge had given up on the idea she would find the detective business too disagreeable to want to continue in it some months ago. He had also come to rely on Victoria, and thought her a rather promising detective. Though he would never admit to such a thing out loud. He would not want such talk going to her head.

"There is a gentleman downstairs wishing to speak to you," Victoria said, having satisfied herself that her uncle was not moping over his failure to solve Houston's murder.

"How intriguing," Bainbridge said, then he paused. "He does not happen to look like a taxman does he?"

"I would not know what such a fellow looked like," Victoria said with a frown. "However, I dealt with your taxes this year, and I am quite certain they were all in order."

"Good," Bainbridge said. "I do not believe there is anyone else I am avoiding just at the moment."

Victoria made a small noise that indicated her impatience.

"Very well, then we ought to meet this person and determine what they want," Bainbridge rose from his desk chair, always a complex operation with his girth.

They both headed downstairs and into the front drawing room, where a man in his forties was whiling the time away as he waited, by studying the paintings on the wall. He was a tall fellow, with a slight unruly crown of fair hair atop his head. He had gone to some pains to try to tame this unruly crop with oil, but his hair had other ideas. When he had removed his hat upon being introduced to Victoria by Mrs Huggins, all his hair had stuck up on end like a scarecrow. It had been a source of some embarrassment to him.

Now he turned to Bainbridge, and revealed a friendly face, though somewhat narrow in appearance which gave him an unhappy similarity to a rat. His smile, however, and general good cheer made up for this unfortunate resemblance.

"You must be Colonel Bainbridge," he said brightly, offering a hand to the colonel. "I am Lancelot Dunbar, of the Shropshire Dunbars."

Bainbridge took his hand and shook it.

"It is a pleasure to meet you, Mr Dunbar. You have already been introduced to my niece, Victoria Bovington."

"Yes, she kindly made me welcome, and said she would fetch you. I do apologise for disturbing you both on a Sunday afternoon. I should not have done so, except this was the only occasion I was able to get into the city and seek you out. I am desperate for your assistance, you see."

"I find, as a detective, it is prudent to be ready to welcome unexpected guests at any time," Bainbridge assured him. "Please do be seated. Has my niece explained she assists me in my cases?"

"Miss Bovington was very clear on the subject," Mr Dunbar said, revealing there had been a slight misunderstanding between them when he first arrived. This happened rather a lot when people failed to appreciate Victoria was just as capable as her uncle. "I will be very grateful if you will both undertake to resolve for me what is quite a peculiar affair for me."

"Do go on," Bainbridge said, intrigued already.

"I reside in a fine old house in Cambridgeshire," Mr Dunbar began. "I moved in a few months ago, following the death of my aunt whose house it was. She has been unwell these last few years and I would try to visit her once a week to see how she was doing. In the final weeks of her life, she was well aware her time was short, and she made me promise over and over, that when I inherited the house I would not sell it.

"The house had been in our family for generations, and I took her to be troubled by the notion of the place she had grown up in, and where her father had grown up, and her grandfather before her, being sold to strangers. As it happened, I was living in a property that was perfectly satisfactory, but which held no strong attraction for me, and I was content to agree to this arrangement."

"There is certainly nothing unusual in such pleas from a person who is dying, and is fondly attached to a place," Bainbridge concurred.

"My aunt was also aware I was to be married this coming winter, and the house will certainly make a fine home to raise a family in. She had met my betrothed, and approved of her. In fact, I believe they had become quite attached to one another. In any case, when my aunt passed away a couple of months ago, I was made aware by the family solicitor that she had indeed left the property, and all her worldly fortune, to me.

"There was just one caveat to my inheritance, which was that I was not to remove anything from the attic. I assumed this referred to any old family belongings that were stored up there, and which my aunt feared might be sold or discarded. I must admit, at the time I was somewhat hurt by the stipulation. I thought my aunt knew me better than to suppose I was the sort of person who would callously get rid of family items."

"I am sure she did not mean it as such," Victoria spoke. "Sometimes, at the end of their days, people become very worried about what will happen to the things they cannot take with them, and the thought of these items simply being disposed of fills their thoughts."

"Yes, you are quite right Miss Bovington. In her last days, my aunt was very concerned about the history of our family, and what would become of everything when she passed on," Mr Dunbar nodded. "However, as it turns out, her stipulation in her will was masking something far more serious than a fear I should sell some old furniture, or Great Great Grandfather's military uniform."

"Ah, this is where we come in, I imagine," Bainbridge was leaning forward in his curiosity.

"Quite," Mr Dunbar nodded. "When I first arrived at the house, my priority was to have an inventory made of everything, and to have a surveyor check the house for all the usual things; damp, woodworm, rot in the rafters. The property is positively ancient and it is constructed largely of wood and plaster, with some later additions in brick.

"The surveyor I employed was from the firm of Blackbird and Strauss, who specialise in historic properties."

"I have heard of them," Bainbridge said. "I believe they are considered very reliable."

"I have no complaints about their work," Mr Dunbar confirmed.

"Due to its size, and historical importance, Mr Blackbird came himself to assess the property. I will become quite distracted if I start to describe the property's history to you, because it is a topic that truly fascinates me. Suffice it to say, it is very old, and has some extremely interesting historic features which Mr Blackbird swiftly identified. Considering its age, it was with some satisfaction I learned from the surveyor that both the ground floor and first floor were in very good condition, with only some minor damp issues, and a chimney that needs some repair work.

"We moved on to the attic, which, until that day, I had never entered. I had never seen any need to and, perhaps feeling a little contrary because of the clause in my aunt's will, I had ignored the space entirely.

"When we entered, I found it a typical attic space, piled with old steamer trunks full of clothes, and household items, along with a selection of old furniture. The attic goes right up into the roof beams, and is only tall enough for a man to stand up in the middle portion. However, it is quite wide to match the width of the house, and certainly spacious. Mr Blackbird went about his work, while I took my time glancing at this and that.

"Certainly it is a treasure trove of family heirlooms, and I should like to properly catalogue the contents some day, but what caught my interest was something at the far end of the attic. Mr Blackbird drew my attention to it when he found it. Situated at the north end of the attic, where the old building meets a modern wing of the house made of stone and brick, he pointed out a small lead box, which I should best describe as a coffer."

"A coffer?" Victoria was intrigued.

"A very small one; I should say it was no more than two feet by one foot," Mr Dunbar explained. "You might almost have supposed it to be a water tank, except it was so tiny. Mr Blackbird pointed it out because he was concerned that one of the beams it sat on appeared to be buckling. When he tested the beam, he discovered it was riddled with woodworm, and thus the lead box was in peril of falling through the ceiling.

"This was the worst area of damage he had found so far, but the discovery of woodworm in one beam indicated the blighters were likely in all of the attic's wooden structure, which would require the attic to be fumigated, and some beams replaced. All the contents would need to be removed prior to this task.

"It was at this point that we both took a closer look at the lead box, as Mr Blackbird wondered if it might be best to remove it immediately. We realised it was screwed to the two beams it perched upon. While examining it, I noticed there was a plaque on one side. It was copper and had tarnished badly, but I was able to rub at it with a handkerchief to make it legible. There was an inscription that rather baffled me. I am almost reluctant to repeat what it said."

"You have brought us this far, Mr Dunbar," Bainbridge spoke keenly. "You cannot leave us in suspense. However remarkable the writing on the plaque is, we would gladly know of it."

Mr Dunbar was relieved by Bainbridge's words and he braced himself to continue.

"At this point, no one aside from myself or Mr Blackbird knew about the lead box and its plaque. Naturally, I assumed my aunt had known of it, and the stipulation in her will may have been directed specifically at this one item. Not that I would ever dream of selling the contents of the house, but I suppose another person might."

"You are tantalising me, Mr Dunbar, what were the mysterious contents?"

Mr Dunbar had been beating about the bush, now it was time to be honest and trust that Bainbridge and Victoria were as understanding as he had heard.

"The plaque was archaic in its wording, so if you please, I shall give you a simplified version," he shrugged, before taking a deep breath. "The sign told us that within the lead box resided the decapitated skull of Oliver Cromwell."

Chapter Two

"I fear I misheard you," Bainbridge said, a frown crossing his face. "Could you repeat that?"

"I assure you, Colonel, you heard me correctly. I said that the little copper plaque states that inside the lead box is the skull of Oliver Cromwell, who won the English Civil War and was Lord Protector, for a brief time, until he died and Charles II was restored to the throne."

Mr Dunbar sat patiently and awaited their response.

"I recall my history," Victoria spoke first. "Oliver Cromwell died in his bed and was buried with the appropriate honours. However, when Charles II returned to the throne, he sought vengeance for the execution of his father, Charles I. He ideally wanted to see Oliver Cromwell tried for treason, but the man had cheated him by dying first. Disgracefully, he ordered Cromwell's body to be exhumed from its rightful grave and hung in chains at Tyburn, and then thrown into a pit. Cromwell's head, however, was removed and displayed on a pike outside Westminster Hall."

"Yes, that is how Cromwell's head became detached from his body. The subsequent history of the skull is murky. There are lots of stories of it being stolen from the pike by loyal followers of Cromwell, or that it fell down and was carried off by a soldier. Popular opinion is that it currently resides with the Wilkinson family of Northamptonshire. Dr Horace Wilkinson purchased the item in 1814," Dunbar added. "Which leaves the very curious matter of the lead box, and my aunt's specific instructions concerning her attic, which strike me as being expressly directed at the preservation of that particular artefact."

Bainbridge had been very quiet during this interlude, Victoria glanced in his direction.

"What are your thoughts?" she asked him.

"I was wondering if you have opened the lead box, Mr Dunbar?"

Dunbar shook his head firmly.

"Heavens, no, I was all for ignoring the thing completely," he winced. "Mr Blackbird also declined opening the box for me, sharing much of my aversion. It remains where we found it, waiting to be moved to repair the beams, but that can be done by the workmen when they arrive."

"Then, I am curious, Mr Dunbar, why have you come to me?"

Dunbar looked embarrassed that he had failed to explain himself sufficiently.

"While I do not personally wish to look inside this box, Mr Blackbird made it plain that I should know its contents, and the value of them, for the sake of insurance purposes. If the head is that of Cromwell, then it could be worth a small fortune, and if someone unscrupulous were to learn of its place in my attic, they might consider trying to steal it. However, he has declined to assist me himself, claiming it is a task better suited to someone who does not have an interest in the item's value."

"Mr Blackbird makes a very wise point," Bainbridge nodded. "Equally, if the box proves empty, considering that Cromwell's head is said to be happily residing with the Wilkinson family, then you have no reason to concern yourself further about the item."

"It would certainly make me feel easier to know it was empty," Dunbar concurred. "I have been living at the house a few weeks now, and ever since the discovery of the box, I find myself lying in bed and staring up at the ceiling imagining it there. I had to change my bedroom arrangements. Originally, I was sleeping in my aunt's bedroom, as it was the only one furnished with a bed. That was immediately beneath the resting place of the skull, so I had the servants move the bed to the far side of the house, into another room, as far away as possible. My aunt's aging butler insists I have quite finished him off with the task."

"I can understand the desire to not sleep beneath a skull," Victoria said, a slight shiver running down her spine as she contemplated the idea. People kept peculiar things in attics, you never quite knew what you would find.

"There is one final eventuality we have not so far considered," Bainbridge spoke.

Dunbar looked at him nervously.

"What is that?" he asked.

"If we open this box and it does contain a skull, yet the skull of Cromwell is plainly established to be kept elsewhere, then whose skull might it be?"

Dunbar went white as a sheet.

"My aunt would not be keeping random skulls in her home," he said firmly. "I am quite sure the box must be empty, and some mistake has occurred. But, you see, I do not wish to open the thing alone. Well, I would rather not open it at all, but Mr Blackbird is correct, I must know its contents. I do not suppose I shall sleep a wink if I avoid opening it, as I will be thinking over all the possibilities.

"I need some reliable and honest witnesses to be with me when the box is opened, who can testify to its contents, just in case anyone were to query my actions. I do not want to accidentally go against the directions of my aunt."

"I fully understand, Mr Dunbar," Bainbridge nodded. "And finding the right sort of witness is difficult. The police will not be interested in a curious family antique after all. However, you might have asked the family solicitor?"

"I did," Dunbar sighed. "He declined. He is an elderly man who informed me flatly he has no intention of taking up gravedigging in his old age. Which was rather unfair, I feel."

"Suggesting that your family solicitor is not entirely sceptical of the idea of your aunt having a skull in her house," Bainbridge observed.

"All quite absurd," Dunbar said hastily. "My aunt was the dearest of creatures. I cannot fathom how she slept all these years with such a thing overhead. She would not say boo to a goose. Why, should she find a dead bird in the garden she would take pains to bury it properly. That was the sort of woman she was."

"The relic is far older than your aunt was," Victoria pointed out. "It may have entered the house long before she was born. She was aware of it as a peculiar family heirloom."

"An heirloom she never mentioned to me," Dunbar looked hurt now. "I thought we were close. I cared a great deal for her, and my weekly visits were never undertaken to secure an inheritance, but were made out of genuine fondness for her. I start to wonder now if she saw things differently, and supposed I was merely marking time until the house was mine."

"Do not judge her so harshly when she cannot counter you," Bainbridge said gently. "It may be your aunt felt you would be upset to learn of the skull, and would refuse to reside in the house at all, which would force the property to be either sold or left to rot."

Victoria agreed with her uncle.

"The clause in her will was perhaps to protect you, rather than to protect the items in the attic. She hoped you would never even know of the existence of the box."

"I *am* rather squeamish about such things," Dunbar admitted. "It is well known within the family that I do not have the stomach for unpalatable items, such as taxidermy. Once, as a boy, I fainted at the sight of a sheep skull. I have always had a very strong aversion to things that remind me of death."

"Had Mr Blackbird not noticed the woodworm, you probably would have remained oblivious to the box's presence," Bainbridge noted. "It would have been left untouched until whomever next inherited the house came across it."

"I suppose you are right," Dunbar nodded. "Will you assist me in this matter? It should only take a few hours of your time, and I shall pay you well for the bother."

"We will gladly assist," Bainbridge told him, always happy to take on a case that would pay well and only required a minimum of effort on his part.

"I am very relieved to hear that," Dunbar said, groaning as he spoke. "I wrote out my address in the hopes you would agree to this. My family solicitor advises me that I shall require a written and signed statement from you both, about your observation of the box being opened and what was inside, so that all will be in order with the will. As long as the box does not leave the house, then I am not breaking any of my aunt's directions."

"Out of curiosity, what would happen if you did break this peculiar attic clause in the will?" Victoria asked. "I assume you have checked this with the family solicitor."

"I have," Dunbar looked morose as he admitted this. "I am

informed that should I depart from my aunt's express wishes, which she had legally outlined in her will, so soon after her death, then I can expect other members of the family to contest my inheritance of the property, should they learn of the matter."

"And the discovery of a skull in one's attic, and its subsequent removal, is the sort of thing difficult to keep completely quiet," Bainbridge understood.

"I will be perfectly honest with you, Colonel, I do not entirely trust the family solicitor. He is heavily in favour of my cousin, and tried to persuade my aunt to see him inherit her home. She was of the opinion that, should this occur, the property would be immediately sold and a proportion of the money would go to our family solicitor."

"That is quite a serious allegation," Bainbridge pointed out. "Your solicitor would be guilty of acting in a biased fashion, if such were the case."

"Certainly Mr Haggerton treads a fine line when it comes to these matters," Dunbar said darkly. "He covers himself by being quick to point out when my actions could void my claim to the will, though I have no doubt he is working behind my back."

Victoria nodded.

"If anyone were to question his scruples, he would say, 'ah, but I informed Mr Dunbar most clearly about what would happen if he broke the directions of the will.' Making it appear he is being perfectly honest, when, truthfully, he is just waiting for you to slip up."

"You see things plainly," Dunbar smiled at her. "I might be wrong, of course, but I have always fancied that Mr Haggerton is a slimy sort of fellow. His family have been solicitors for three generations, and the original Mr Haggerton looked after my great grandfather. That is why the current member of that dynasty is retained by us."

"It also explains why he was so reluctant to assist in opening the box," Bainbridge concluded. "Most solicitors would agree to help, even if they did not wish to, because they felt it their duty. His refusal did strike me as odd."

"I am afraid he may not be alone in his disapproval of me," Dunbar said anxiously. "You recall I mentioned my aunt's butler?"

"The fellow you 'quite finished off,'" Victoria replied.

"Yes. Mr Jennings," Dunbar's face took on an unhappy expression. "He served my aunt loyally, and was devoted to her, of that I am certain. However, he too favoured my cousin over myself for the inheritance of the house. My cousin comes through the male line of the family. His father was my aunt's brother. My grandfather was somewhat radical for his age, in that he settled one of his main pieces of property upon his daughter rather than his son.

"You see, his daughter – my aunt – shared his passion for natural history. She worked as his assistant, transcribing his notes on various topics, helping with research and proofing any papers or books he submitted to be published. They shared quite a bond, and she never found another man who was interesting enough to take her away from her father's work. She told me that directly.

"Her father made careful provision for her in his will, so that she could continue to live independently, and pursue her studies, which she did, right until the end. My uncle and my cousin indulged rather than approved of these arrangements, believing that one day the house and the estate would fall back into their hands, when my aunt passed.

"My understanding is that Jennings, who served my grandfather before my aunt, was in correspondence with my uncle and cousin. He probably still is. He wrote to them of matters concerning my aunt, but failed to realise just how close I had become to the old woman. You can imagine his shock, as much as my cousin's, when the will was read out, and I was named heir to the house and land."

"Where do you fit in this complex family arrangement?" Bainbridge asked.

"My father was the youngest child of the family. He went into the army and sadly perished when I was just a boy. It was malarial fever, they say."

"Ah, yes, I have seen that take down strong young men before now," Bainbridge said sadly.

"I was raised by my mother and her parents. I lost touch with my father's side of the family during my childhood, but as a grown man I wanted to learn more about my father, and so reached out to his brother and sister. It was only my aunt who responded to my appeal and that was how we came to be in touch."

"I begin to see how you are considered an outsider by your cousin. Someone who has slipped in and stolen what he deems rightfully his," Bainbridge said with a soft smile on his lips.

"That was never my intention," Dunbar assured him. "I merely wished to learn about my father. My mother never remarried, and was devoted to his memory. She spoke of him in the manner all people do of someone deceased who was dearly loved, ironing out his flaws, polishing up his strengths. My aunt gave me a far more honest picture of him, and it made me think of him as an actual person, rather than the fantasy my mother had painted."

"Yes, that often happens," Bainbridge said sagely. "Well, I can promise you Mr Dunbar, we shall help you in this matter, and provide the witnesses you require to stave off any malicious complaints from your cousin."

"Thank you," Dunbar was delighted. "Will you come down tomorrow? There is a train station not far from the house, and I shall have the carriage sent to collect you."

"Expect us tomorrow," Bainbridge agreed. "It shall be an

interesting excursion, no doubt."

"Not too interesting," Dunbar said, a touch nervously. "I am sure it is just an empty box."

"Of course," Bainbridge reassured him.

Chapter Three

First thing the following morning, Victoria and Bainbridge set out by train for the home of Mr Dunbar. All the talk from the day before about the mystery of the skull in the lead box, had got them thinking about the history of England, and the strange events of the English Civil War. Oliver Cromwell was the sort of historical figure you learned about at school. His story was taught in history classes, and he had been paraded as a reformer, as someone who had seen the way the world was, and decided it needed to be altered, and that he was the man to do the altering.

Both Victoria and Bainbridge were familiar with British history, and the role Oliver Cromwell had played in radically altering the status quo. They also knew the many legends that circulated about his skull and what happened to it – or, rather, what supposedly happened to it – when it fell from the pike it had been placed upon. To suppose that it was sitting in someone's attic, (a place it certainly should not have been) tucked into a lead box was peculiar, to say the least. But not just that. It made you wonder about the Dunbar family. At what point in the Dunbars' history had the skull suddenly entered their lives? Had it been bought? Had it been somehow snuck into the house? Were previous members of the Dunbar family secret parliamentarians?

Of course, none of this would matter if the box proved to be empty, and Bainbridge was hopeful *it would* be empty. It would solve a lot of issues for Mr Dunbar, and it would mean he could rest easy, and not be concerned that the former Lord Protector's head was residing in his attic.

They arrived at the home of Mr Dunbar in brilliant sunshine. Though the summer was growing late, and sometimes in the evening there was just the hint of the coming autumn, during the day it was hot and beautiful. The trees had yet to start to turn to that brilliant orange of autumn. They knew there were still many more days of gorgeous sunshine ahead before they had to start thinking about the coming winter.

Mr Dunbar's home was as he had described it; a fine example of the late medieval period, with additions added in the Georgian and Victorian period. It was largely timber built, the beams blackened with age, and the windows small with leaded panes. The roof must have originally been thatched, but now it was replaced with tiles – far more practical and fire resistant. The house sprawled across the garden, as so many old houses did that had been added to over the generations, in a haphazard fashion. It looked magnificent, and despite what Mr Dunbar had said about getting a surveyor in, it was clear it had been well maintained by his aunt. The gardens that surrounded it were in that hazy, overblown stage of late summer bloom. Everything looked as if it had seen its best, and was now just putting on a show for the sake of it. It was truly idyllic and the sort of property that you could imagine being sketched in an etching for a magazine such as *The Strand*.

Mr Dunbar had greeted them at the train station with the family carriage, as he had stated he would. It was rather old and a little bit worn around the edges, but it still ran beautifully, a luxurious item that clearly had cost a considerable fortune in its day. He was proud to say that his grandfather had sat in the same carriage, and had even travelled up to London in it.

Mr Dunbar had a lot of stories about his father and grandfather, who he had only recently learned about himself. Like many people who have suddenly acquired new family members, Mr Dunbar was keen to talk about them and reveal what he knew. Having never known his father as a boy, he was excited now to regale Bainbridge and Victoria about all the things his father had done. His aunt had clearly collected many stories, and it was plain Mr Dunbar was besotted with the family he had once thought he had lost.

It was also obvious that he loved the house. The second they were on the drive and heading towards the main doors, he was pointing out its features. He was telling them about a window where someone long ago had scratched their initials into the glass with a diamond ring. No one remembered who this person was, nor which particular family member they had been, but it was still exciting to see those scratches, to know that someone had walked down the same corridors centuries before Mr Dunbar did. He pointed out where trailing roses grew up the side of the house, and remarked that they had been planted by his grandmother. He told them their variety, and how his aunt would pluck roses from them in the summer, arranging them on the table for her father.

Then he told them about his plans for the future of the house, and what he hoped to do with it once he had married and his wife had moved in. He longed for a large family of his own. He hoped that they would grow up in this beautiful place, running across the lawns, enjoying the history of the home and having a childhood as idyllic and glorious as was possible.

It was nice to see that Mr Dunbar was not terribly distraught about the strange find in his attic, and that it hadn't completely ruined his enjoyment of the property. It would have been a shame if a house that he clearly loved had been so tarnished in his eyes that he couldn't enjoy it anymore.

Once they were inside the house, he tried to tell them a little bit about his aunt. He had already explained how she had loved history, and geology, and botany, and all manner of sciences, and had been assistant to his grandfather. He showed them a room where there was a collection of stones and other old artefacts that she had gathered from the garden. She had labelled and catalogued them herself. Dunbar said he had yet to find out if she had correctly dated them, but he was confident she had.

"My aunt was a woman ahead of her time," he told them. "I think you would have liked her, especially you, Miss Bovington. I see much of her in you. A woman who knows her own mind and wants to make her mark on this world without having to acquire a husband to prove herself. Yes, I think she would have admired you, and you would have respected her."

Having now seen much of the work that Dunbar's aunt had done during the course of her lifetime, Victoria was inclined to agree with him. While some of the labelling was old fashioned, it was clear that his aunt had had an inquiring mind, and was not to be stifled by the usual expectations of the day. It still raised a strange question mark over what a skull was doing in the attic, however.

Mr Dunbar offered them tea and refreshments. Bainbridge was not going to refuse this delight, though Victoria was quite keen to get on with the investigation. Mr Dunbar had his butler bring the tea, which meant that Bainbridge and Victoria could get a good look at the man. Mr Jennings was a fellow in his seventies. He had first started at the house as a young boy working for Mr Dunbar's grandfather, and then he had taken over from the former butler. He had worked for Dunbar's grandfather and then his aunt. The man had a surly appearance which had not softened with age. He had a great crop of white hair on his head and he rather reminded Victoria of Mr Dunbar in some regards, though she doubted there was any family connection. Mr Jennings scowled at them, and it was apparent he did not like the fact they were there. He would be quite glad if they all left. He put the tea things down with near enough a slam, and then stalked out.

"You could have an issue here with him," said Bainbridge, nodding in the direction of the departing butler.

Mr Dunbar merely shrugged.

"What can I possibly do about it? It would be unseemly to let him go at his age, he would never get another position. It would be quite cruel."

"You mean to say you will just put up with his attitude?" asked Victoria.

Mr Dunbar considered her comment.

"I suppose that is what I mean, yes," he said. "I just can't see fit to cast him out. He did serve my aunt loyally. She was very fond of him, and really, after a while, you do get used to his disdain. I don't think he would ever actually do anything to hurt me as such. He just likes to show that he disapproves of me."

"What about your other servants?" Bainbridge asked.

"I have no complaint about them. Most of them are younger than Mr Jennings. Unfortunately, many of the servants were quite the family antiques in their own right. I say that in the nicest possible way. Over time, they have either had to retire or simply passed away. My aunt gradually got new people in, though I feel she never quite settled to the new faces. It's hard when you have known people all your life to suddenly find yourself with these strangers in your home, and trying to trust them as well as you would your old servants. Dare I say Mr Jennings was the glue that held it all together, and for that I am truly grateful to him. He made sure that my aunt's dotage was as easy and peaceful as possible. Things could have been much worse without his steady hand at the metaphorical rudder."

"However, he favours your cousin," said Victoria. "That must make things awkward."

"I am sure things will settle down with time," Mr Dunbar said. "I am quite prepared to stick with him, and prove to him that I am a worthy occupant of this house. I think he just needs to get to know me a little better."

"You are an optimist, Mr Dunbar, and that is a most noble thing," Bainbridge said "I admire a man who can keep his head under such circumstances"

"I do not think I quite understand you," Mr Dunbar said. "You seem to think this is far more serious than I do."

"It is just that a man's house is meant to be his private kingdom, if you will, and being beholden to disagreeable servants is quite a challenge. I do not think you fully appreciate just how difficult this situation might become, especially if you are correct and certain servants are working for your cousin."

"I think you are being rather hasty with that judgement, Bainbridge," Dunbar said. "I do not think Jennings' intent is truly malicious. And really, there is nothing much he can do. I am legally entitled to this house as long as I abide by the clauses my aunt put into her will."

"As you say," Bainbridge nodded amenably. "I am sure you are quite correct and that Jennings will not cause any bother once he settles into you as the new owner."

Victoria heard the slight hesitation in her uncle's voice, and she knew what he was thinking. Jennings and the solicitor were all working against Mr Dunbar, and he seemed to think that was perfectly fine. He didn't seem to appreciate that if people were cunning and conniving enough, they could do a man out of his inheritance. If it had been her, Victoria would have instantly replaced Jennings. At least then she could have known that no secrets were being taken from the house straight back to Mr Dunbar's cousin. But it wasn't up to her, and Mr Dunbar did seem quite content to leave things as they were.

She supposed that she ought to call him naïve. It was a gentle, kind naivety, but still one that could end up costing him dearly.

The refreshments fully restored Bainbridge. He was a man of great stomach, and he regularly needed to be fed to be in his prime mystery solving mode. Now he was suitably restored, he was keen to get on with the investigation. They only intended to be at the house for the day, and already it was growing close to noon. He did not intend to miss dinner at home. Mrs Huggins had promised him it would be a cooked chicken with his favourite dumplings.

"Now would seem to be a good time to have a look at this lead box," Bainbridge observed.

He was putting down his cup, now utterly drained of liquid. They had been served biscuits with the tea, and they had been most delightful. He wondered if he could acquire the recipe for Mrs Huggins, and if he could find a way of giving it to her without causing offence. She could be odd when he brought her new recipes home, as if he was implying her cooking was not up to standard.

"You are quite right Bainbridge, we have wasted so much time already. We should head upstairs at once. It is really quite easy to get into the attic. It does not have one of those terribly narrow entrances with a ladder. No, no, there is a full staircase. It is quite sophisticated."

They followed Mr Dunbar out of the sitting room, and up the first flight of stairs. The house wound around different corridors and there were steps here and there, that suddenly sprang out at you and took you by surprise. They were taken along the first floor to a door that could have been just a cupboard, but when it was opened it revealed another flight of stairs.

"This is the way to the attic," Dunbar told them.

Then he escorted them up and into the spacious attic space. While the pitch of the roof meant that only the central part was able to be walked in upright, the dimensions of the attic were certainly impressive, and there was plenty of space for all the furniture and other items that had been stored there over the years.

Dunbar took them to the very end of the attic. He pointed to an object mounted onto the beams, and then he said in a voice that was filled with mild horror.

"This, my friends, is the box. And now comes the dreadful part. Opening it."

Chapter Four

Bainbridge always took things methodically. It was his mantra that if you rushed, you missed something, so when he saw the box before him, he didn't immediately jump to open it. Instead, he took his time examining it. Quite obviously, it was a lead box – nothing exciting there as such. The lead had been soldered down the edges, but the lid appeared to be moveable. The small copper plaque which Mr Dunbar had mentioned earlier, was present and he read it again. It did not enlighten him any further. Clearly, whoever had written it was quite convinced the box contained Cromwell's head.

The box was nondescript. Bainbridge examined it thoroughly, but there were no particular clues as to its age or origins. Lead boxes are lead boxes, and it could have been made at any point in the last several centuries. Its position on the beams was curious; it had clearly been placed to avoid putting too much weight in one area, and it fitted the exact spacing of the beams, suggesting it had been made bespoke. That implied some sort of planning had been involved when the box had been commissioned.

What did any of that mean? It seemed to suggest that whoever had devised the idea for this box had done so because they wanted to place an object the shape and size of a human skull up here, and they knew the exact place they wanted to put it. Did that indicate that some long-dead Dunbar had planned to steal Cromwell's head and hide it secretly in the attic? Did that mean one forgotten member of the Dunbar family had been a loyal parliamentarian, who could not bear to see the Lord Protector's skull put on public display? Might there be some distance connection between Cromwell and the Dunbar family?

With this in mind, Bainbridge concluded the only option was to prise open the lid of the box, and to examine its contents. They were all rather hopeful it would be empty, especially Mr Dunbar and Victoria.

Victoria was uncomfortable around dead bodies. It was the one thing that made being a detective very unpleasant for her. She was not so disturbed if the deceased were recently dead, unless they had suffered a grim death, (for instance, there was a lot of blood splashed about or body parts were missing) then she tended to go rather faint and had to sit down. But when it came to corpses that had been 'hanging around' for a while, that might be slightly mummified, or just looked a bit decayed, she preferred not to have to gaze upon them. She had already experienced one mummified body in a previous case and it had stuck in her mind. She still sometimes closed her eyes at night and saw visions of the corpse huddled up, darkened, withered, shrivelled. It was not something conducive to a good night's sleep.

Bainbridge looked at the lead lid and noted it had no hinge. It was intended it should lift completely off. He also noted it had not been soldered in place. It therefore should be relatively easy for him to lift it. He felt under the rim and noticed a slight gap between the lid and the top of the box. However, having been in the same position for numerous years – how many it was impossible to guess – the lid had sunk in on itself and become quite stuck. Winters of intense cold, and summers of muggy heat had caused the lead to warp, shrink, then expand again, and generally settle tightly in place.

After determining that he was not going to open the thing with his fingers alone, Bainbridge fumbled in his pocket and drew out a pocketknife. He extracted one of the smoother blades that wasn't too sharp or liable to stab him in the finger, and then he gently wedged it into the gap between the box edge and the lid, and wiggled it. Slowly, he felt years of dust, debris and dirt give way. There was a slight popping noise, very faint but audible, and when he moved the knife a fraction up, he was sure the lid moved as well. He worked his way all around, clearing out the small gap between lid and box, and then he tried again to lever it up. Even with his efforts, the lid was a tight fit and did not budge.

"Vicky you will need to lift that end while I lift this end," he said to his niece.

Victoria gave him a stern look.

"I do not think that would be appropriate," she said. "It is, after all, Mr Dunbar's box."

Mr Dunbar looked sheepish. He stared at the box and wondered why he had been put into such a position. Why had he, of all the people in this world, found himself the unhappy possessor of a skull in his attic?

Bainbridge glanced at him. The look was meaningful. Dunbar resigned himself to helping out. Crouching on the opposite side of the box to Bainbridge, he bent down and put his fingers underneath the lid. It was a very narrow gap, and he could barely get his fingernails underneath it.

"I will count to three and then we will lift together."

Bainbridge counted relatively slowly. Well, it was Bainbridge.

"One. Two. Three."

Together, they lifted the lid of the box. A cloud of dust spewed out, and Victoria took a quick step back in case there was something noxious spilling out of the box. She had heard stories about people going to Egypt, and other exotic countries, to dig in old tombs, and then being overcome by some sort of ancient miasma, that had filtered out from the cavernous ruins.

As it was, it seemed that whatever spewed out of the box was merely age-old dust, and possibly a little bit of mummified skull. When the lid was raised, and the dust had settled, both Dunbar and Bainbridge glanced into the box. Bainbridge was eager. Dunbar was hopeful he would see nothing. Victoria discreetly held back.

Disappointingly, within the box there was another one, made of wood. Their curiosity was still unsated. Dunbar audibly sighed.

"I really was braced for the discovery just then," he said. "I don't know if I can go through all that tension and suspense again."

Bainbridge tutted at him.

"Really, man, you must get a hold of yourself. Your nervousness is unbecoming of a gentleman."

Dunbar looked a fraction hurt.

"Well, yes, I suppose I should be a bit more enthusiastic about these things. No, not enthusiastic. What is the word? I should be steadier. Steady nerves are what a man needs. I ought not to be shrinking back like a woman."

Upon hearing this, Victoria felt her own pang of hurt. She rather fancied her uncle had made the slight against Dunbar as a backhanded way of making a slight at her. Feeling that her integrity as a detective was being impinged, she took a purposeful step forward, and crouched by the box.

"Enough of all this. I shall open the next box."

She dug into the lead box and removed the wooden container, which came out quite smoothly. It was a fraction smaller than the original box, and clearly had been made purposefully to fit it. The double interior was starting to look rather like a miniature coffin arrangement, at least in the manner in which the boxes nestled into each other.

"This reminds me of old medieval tombs," Bainbridge said. "If you were extremely wealthy, you would have two coffins. A lead one and a wooden one, one inside the other. That way you could be sure you would be preserved for the Day of Judgement. In fact, the Romans did something similar, if I recall. There might even have been some found in London, though I could be making that up. It all rather suggests that within this box is something rather special."

"Can you call skulls special?" Dunbar asked.

"A skull is rather special to the owner of said skull. By that I mean, our own skulls are rather important to us, if you think about it. So it rather depends on what you define as special," Bainbridge rambled.

He was starting to enjoy himself.

Victoria was tired of all this chat. She felt everybody was deferring the moment when the box would be opened and reveal its contents. She now put her fingers under the lid, which in this case was hinged, and lifted it. Unlike the lead lid, this one did not resist her movement, and she opened it smoothly. What she saw inside made her regret being so eager. There was a grinning skull leering at her.

"Oh my!" said Mr Dunbar.

He then promptly subsided into a half faint, falling back against a beam in the attic, and clunking his own skull rather heavily. Bainbridge shook his head and glanced at his niece.

"Anything to suggest this is the head of Oliver Cromwell?" He asked.

Victoria was endeavouring not to look too hard at the skull. It was blackened, and still retained some of the skin that had formerly covered the face. There were no eyes, just hollows, and the mouth had dropped open so she could see all the teeth within. There were still some wisps of hair attached to the scalp.

"Well, I can say this, it is a skull. However, there is no label to determine whose skull," Victoria said coldly.

Bainbridge moved closer to the box. He peered in at the blackened skull and studied it calmly. It could have been anybody's skull, as far as he could tell. There was really nothing to determine who had formerly owned it. This *could* be the head of the former Lord Protector, and if it was, that was quite a significant thing. And yet, it could just as easily be the head of any poor unfortunate.

Dunbar was recovering his senses. He sat up and looked at them shyly.

"Sorry about that," he said. "It was just something of a shock to see there was a skull there, a real skull. I was really banking on that box being empty."

Bainbridge said nothing, rather feeling Mr Dunbar needed to pull himself together.

"How do we go about determining if it really is the genuine skull of Oliver Cromwell?" Victoria asked, distracting him.

"I will admit that is slightly novel to me," Bainbridge concurred. "I have never had to identify a skull before, at least not in this way. It will require a little bit of thought."

Bainbridge rubbed his chin as he mused on the matter.

"I suppose the correct way to start would be to see if there are any papers in the house that indicate how the family might be connected to Cromwell. If we could find, say, a paper that indicated a prior member of the family had strong connections to the Lord Protector, and that they might have gone out of their way to rescue his head, that would be a start in proving this was his skull. Equally, if we perhaps found a document of sale which indicated that this had been bought as Oliver Cromwell's skull, we would have a good means of identifying it."

"I thought that the real Oliver Cromwell's skull was in the possession of a different family?" Victoria said. "Or should I say the skull that is said to be the real Oliver Cromwell's skull?"

"That does make things complicated," Bainbridge agreed. "We would need some very strong evidence to prove this *is* the skull of Oliver Cromwell, if our claims are to be taken seriously"

Dunbar was sitting up now and staring at them. He looked uneasy.

"If this isn't the skull of Oliver Cromwell, what would that mean exactly?" He asked.

Victoria looked at him as if that should have been somewhat obvious. Bainbridge, however, patiently replied.

"If this is not the skull of Oliver Cromwell, then we do have a real mystery on our hands. People's heads don't just suddenly turn up in attics. Someone had to take this head off a person, either before or after they were dead, and put it in this box before hiding it up here. The question is why? I mean, if it is Oliver Cromwell's skull, we have a very good reason. But if it's someone else's skull, than either this is an attempted case of forgery or something more sinister has occurred."

The colour was slowly draining out of Dunbar's face.

"What do you mean by sinister," he asked uneasily.

"He means that if this is not the skull of Oliver Cromwell, then your family has in its possession the skull of a complete stranger, and we have to ask how it ended up here. Was he murdered, for instance?"

Dunbar had just about got his head around the idea that some distant relative might have been involved in the theft of the skull, due to some forgotten family loyalties to the parliamentarian cause. He could not get his head around the idea that there might be a murderer in the family, someone who had hidden a skull up in the attic, and then then spread the rumour that it was Oliver Cromwell's to mask their crime. He was starting to feel a little faint again.

"What... What do we do now?" He asked.

"There is only one thing we can do," Bainbridge said. "We do as I first suggested. We look into your family papers. We try to find out who might have obtained this skull and brought it into the house. We do our best and, at the end of the day, if we cannot prove that this is Oliver Cromwell's skull, then perhaps the easiest option will be to put it back in this box and to forget about it. After all, if it's been here centuries, the odds of finding out who it really belonged to are very slim, and any murderer is long dead."

"Surely we are just giving up on justice if we do that?" Victoria said. "This poor person did not deserve to have their head put in a box, whether they are Oliver Cromwell or not, they ought to be buried decently."

Dunbar was still struggling to comprehend all that had occurred to him in the last couple of days, let alone the last hour. He ran his hand over his eyes.

"I think I could do with another cup of tea," he said.

Bainbridge smiled cheerfully.

"That sounds positively delightful," he declared.

Chapter Five

Dunbar needed to consume quite a quantity of tea to recover from his misadventure in the attic. They had brought the wooden box downstairs, and it was now set upon the dining room table. He looked upon it, wondering about its contents, frowning as he considered his family reputation, and what must have gone on in the past.

"I honestly don't think anybody in the family was particularly involved in politics," he said after a moment. "I admit I don't know much about my family history, but I like to think I have a clear understanding of what sort of people we were."

Bainbridge gave him a strange look.

"Mr Dunbar, no one truly knows their ancestors. It is impossible to do so. And you have barely known yours for, what, a matter of months? You can hardly make a judgement about what sort of people they were based upon that."

"I appreciate what you are saying, but I honestly believe that my family wouldn't be involved in something such as this. It just isn't the sort of thing that the Dunbars would do."

Bainbridge knew when he was fighting a losing battle, so he didn't try to answer back.

"That is all well and good, Mr Dunbar, but sitting before us we have a box that contains a skull, which has been identified by a small copper plaque to be the head of Oliver Cromwell," Victoria pointed out. "Whatever your feelings on your family, surely the evidence before your eyes indicates that someone, at some point, had an unhealthy interest in decapitated heads. To put it simply, they either stole away Cromwell's head to protect it, or they bought it."

Mr Dunbar looked quite bleak at this assessment. He knew she was right. He knew in his heart of hearts that somewhere, back in the mists of time, one of his ancestors had purchased the skull, or had stolen it, and placed it in the attic. He just didn't want to believe that sorry truth. It was not something he would ever do, and if he would not do it, then how could he suppose a family member would? It seemed to throw off everything he knew about himself and all his ancestors. It especially threw him off about his aunt.

"My aunt knew the secret to all this," he said after a moment. "If she was still alive, we could ask her all about it. Of course, she did not want me to know about it while she was alive. Maybe she thought I wouldn't take the house on if I did."

"She probably had a better understanding of you then you give her credit for," Bainbridge said, though not unkindly. "Having skulls hidden in one's house is not a thing that everybody wants, or needs, or desires. I should say it's far more normal to dislike having such a thing in one's home, than it is to desire it. You aunt must have had a very important reason for wanting to keep this box secure and safe."

"Do you suppose she feared that her other nephew would sell it, if he was able to get hands on this house?" Victoria asked.

Bainbridge considered this idea.

"It would seem reasonable to suppose that an option. I have to assume that Miss Dunbar's brother was fully aware of the skull, and its significance. He may even have made mention of selling it, or disposing of it in some way, that had caused his sister to be quite concerned. Of course, it could just be true that she was worried her nephew would sell this house immediately he inherited it, and she did not want to see the family home in use by strangers. But it does make one wonder about this whole affair."

They all found themselves staring at the box. Its lid was closed again, and it sat between the tea things. It looked quite innocuous. It could have been one of those old tea chests people used, to keep the tea leaves locked away from the servants.

"Mr Dunbar have you examined the family library for any evidence concerning this relic?" Bainbridge asked next, getting back to business.

Mr Dunbar shook his head.

"I have to say it has been such a shock. I never even considered looking in the library until you mentioned it earlier. I imagine my aunt kept papers. She was quite the correspondent, and surely my grandfather would have kept something with his keen interest in history. In fact, I would be truly surprised if there wasn't something up there."

"Then that is where we need to go to next," Bainbridge said. "We need to take a good look at the family archives, and determine who precisely brought this skull here, and whether there is a case to be made for it being Cromwell's head."

"That is all very well," Mr Dunbar said, looking anxious. "But there is one other thing that troubles me. I cannot have this skull in my house and expect to be able to sleep a wink. I would most appreciate it if you, Bainbridge, would take the skull with you when you leave, and look after it until we can determine quite what its history is, and whether it should remain at the house."

Victoria's eyes grew wide as she heard this statement. The last thing she wanted was a skull in her home, sitting somewhere, and grinning its awful grin. It was bad enough sitting next to it when it was in someone else's house. All the time she was drinking tea, she found herself looking at the box, and envisioning the skull within; its hollow eyes seemed to be pointing at her, even though she knew they were not, and in fact were staring straight up at the lid of the box. She could have sworn there was a strange aura around the thing. She was not one to particularly believe in ghosts, but there was definitely something odd, and rather too gothic, about the whole experience she was now enduring.

"I am quite happy to do that if you wish," Bainbridge declared, earning a scowl from his niece. "But you have to be very sure about this. I do not want to go against your aunt's wishes. Remember, even just by me taking this skull for a short period of time, it could be seen as you invalidating the conditions of her will."

Mr Dunbar considered this carefully and then groaned.

"You make a very sound point. I suppose I am stuck with the thing, aren't I?"

Victoria keenly piped up.

"I think it is advisable you keep the skull here. If we were to take it, I think it would encourage certain people to press a claim against you and this house, and try to declare you shouldn't be here. It is much better if it stays with you."

Dunbar pulled a face, but he knew they were right. He couldn't risk his cousin finding any means to start a legal battle against him for the property. Despite his earlier words about his butler, Jennings, and how he trusted him, he had to admit that were the old boy to find out he had sent the skull somewhere else, he would surely pass the information straight on to Dunbar's cousin, and thus begin a terrible legal conundrum. No help would be afforded by the family solicitor, seeing as he was also on the side of Dunbar's cousin. It was all very, very complicated, and somewhat overwhelming.

Dunbar dropped his head into his hands. Bainbridge was distracted, thinking of other ways they could find out the identity of the skull, and already contemplating the mystery ahead of them. He was far too interested in that, to notice Dunbar's demoralised demeanour.

"I wonder if Mr Jennings knows anything about this skull?" He said suddenly.

"The butler?" Victoria remarked.

"Well, he has been with the family an awfully long time, and if the old Mr Dunbar knew of the skull, then the butler would presumably have heard about it. Butlers hear all sorts of things, they are rather like confidants to their masters. We should ask Jennings."

Dunbar did not react to this notion.

"Do you believe that to be a good idea?" Victoria nudged him.

Dunbar lifted his head slowly.

"Sorry, what were you saying? I rather got absorbed in my own thoughts."

"My uncle suggested that we talk to your butler," Victoria explained patiently. "In case he knows anything about this mystery. Perhaps the old Mr Dunbar confided in him at some point, or maybe your aunt. He was in their service, and very loyal to them for years, after all."

Dunbar meekly nodded his head. He didn't have the energy to argue with them. If they wanted to speak to his butler, so be it.

"Don't expect much of a straight answer from him," he warned. "Jennings is a strange kettle of fish."

They rang the bell, and the butler appeared. He glanced briefly at the box on the table, but did not seem to recognise it. This was either good play acting or he really didn't know about the skull. Bainbridge was the one to address him.

"Mr Jennings, I want to ask you about this box and its contents."

Jennings said nothing. His motto was that unless someone asked you a direct question, you didn't respond – at least if the person was anybody who had been invited to the house by Mr Dunbar. His feelings for his new employer were weak at best. At worst, they could be described as disagreeable, perhaps even hostile, but only on a bad day. He would never do anything to directly harm Mr Dunbar. However, he did feel that the young man had rather inserted himself into the family, and that the house should have gone to his cousin. Jennings was a man of propriety, and he disliked the fact the house seemed to be going in a sideways trajectory in its manner of inheritance.

"Are you aware of what is inside this box?" Bainbridge asked the butler.

Jennings frowned.

"I cannot say I am, Sir. I do not believe I have seen it before."

"Do you spend much time up in the attic, among all the old family antiques?" Bainbridge tried instead.

"I sometimes go up to look for things." Jennings answered. "When my mistress was alive, she would sometimes send me up to look for old photo albums or books. Occasionally, she wanted things brought down for special events, such as the big silver soup tureen at Christmas. Other than that, I wouldn't say I spent considerable time up there."

"But you must have been aware of that large lead box sitting on the beams?" Bainbridge suggested.

Jennings was cautious.

"I was aware it existed, Sir."

"Had you ever been told what was inside it?"

Jennings' frown became deeper.

"It was not something we ever particularly discussed," he answered.

"When you say *we,* do you mean yourself and your mistress, or yourself and the old Mr Dunbar?" Bainbridge asked.

"Both," Jennings replied.

Finding the butler recalcitrant, and feeling sure that he knew more than he was letting on, Bainbridge decided to push further.

"Would you mind opening this box for me, Mr Jennings?" He asked.

The butler stepped forward. If he was at all suspicious about the contents of the box, or had any inkling of what they might be, he did not let on in his manner. He was composed and professional as always. He took the lid in both hands and lifted it smoothly. He might have been lifting the lid on a box containing silver cutlery, or some other precious item that he intended to lay out on the table. When his eyes alighted on the skull, which happened to be sideways on to him and grinning upwards, he said nothing, though there might have been a very slight hint of the colour draining from his face. It was reminiscent of the way Dunbar had reacted when he had seen the skull for the first time.

"I do believe it is a skull," Jennings said in a calm voice.

"You cannot tell us anything about it then?" Bainbridge asked.

"I can inform you, quite plainly, that it neither belongs to my mistress or the late Mr Dunbar. Other than that, I do not believe I can assist you, Sir."

With the same care as he had opened the box, Jennings restored the lid. Then he stepped back.

"If that is all, Sir, I shall go back to attending to my duties. I always have an awful lot to do, and there is dinner to be considered."

Dunbar finally looked up and noticed his servant.

"Yes, yes, Jennings, you must have lots to do. Oh, by the way, Bainbridge, I did have this idea while I was sitting here, and the more I consider it, the more I like it."

Victoria looked at Dunbar with an uneasy gaze. She wondered what he was contemplating now, especially after his previous suggestion they take the skull home with them.

"I was thinking that it is a considerable distance for you to travel backwards and forwards from here to Norwich, and ridiculous for you to do it every single day. Therefore, how about you and your niece remain here? As my guests?" Dunbar persisted. "It would give me some peace of mind to know there were other people in the house who knew about this thing."

He indicated the skull.

"And it would make your lives a lot easier."

Victoria surmised from this statement, that Mr Dunbar did not care to be alone in the house with the skull. She was less than pleased to think that she would also be in a house where a skull was resident. Bainbridge, however, thought it was a commendable idea, as it would save on a lot of travel.

"I find the idea most agreeable, Mr Dunbar," he said. "If you are so inclined as to set us up as your guests, I am quite happy to remain. What do you say, Vicky?"

Victoria felt that she was unable to refuse the invitation, for fear she would have to reveal her own concerns about sleeping in a house where there was a skull. That didn't seem very professional for someone who was trying to be a detective.

"It is a perfectly reasonable idea," she said, noting that her uncle had a slight smirk on his face, and suspecting he knew exactly what she was thinking. "It will make things most convenient."

"That is a relief," Mr Dunbar said, sighing. "Well, Jennings, you need to make up two guest rooms that will keep you busy.

Jennings gave them all a sour look, and then departed the room.

Chapter Six

"Why did you agree to stay here?" Victoria complained to her uncle.

They were now in the library on the first floor. It was a spacious room with many windows, and was one of the newer additions to the house. Along two of the walls there were tall bookcases that stretched up to the ceiling. It was not as full a library as the one Bainbridge had at home, but the sort of thing you would expect a well-established family to have. Many of the books were collector's pieces, that you would buy in a lot to fill the shelves, and make it look as though you were a great reader. However, there was one section that contained family journals, papers, and other documents important to the Dunbars.

Mr Dunbar had shown them this section, explaining he had only discovered it the other day. They had gathered up as many documents and journals from the shelves as they could hold, and carried them to the table. They proved to be a mixed bag of paperwork, everything from old family diaries to recipe books, and one was an account book from the 1700s, which listed such things as how much had been paid for a Chippendale sofa, and the cost for a year's worth of wheat for the family.

Among this complex assortment, they hoped to discover the clue to the mystery of the skull. Mr Dunbar had left them alone for a while, saying that he needed to lie down as he had a headache coming on. Apparently, this was a complaint that regularly afflicted him. Though Victoria and Bainbridge had not said anything to each other, they were both thinking that Mr Dunbar was a man prone to nerves. The very last sort of man you would wish a random skull upon.

"I agreed to stay here because it seemed the most practical solution," Bainbridge told his niece. "For a start, we don't have to worry about travelling backwards and forwards by train, which was going to take up considerable time, and waste our energy. I also think that Mr Dunbar needs us here. I think we can both agree he is not the sort of man who could be termed courageous. He needs a little helping hand in this matter, or else he may just completely fall apart."

Bainbridge said this all rather calmly, and matter of fact. Victoria considered his words.

"I suppose I have to agree with you. After all, not many gentlemen would wander away and leave strangers among the family archives with complaints of a headache."

"In fairness to him, he may be one of these poor folks blighted by the terrible migraine. Which I am informed is quite an affliction."

"I suppose therefore we are stuck here," Victoria sighed, resigning herself to her fate.

"You are being rather grim about everything," Bainbridge protested. "This is just another case, another mystery to be solved. Why does it seem to have affected you so?"

Victoria had to admit she was not sure herself; there was something deeply disturbing about the skull, and it was playing on her mind.

"Perhaps it is just the fact that whatever the outcome of our investigation, we are left with a man's head in a box, and what are we to do with it?"

"We have to do our best to determine the rightful owner, and by that I mean the person who had this head when they were alive. Then we will decide where it should go next. Personally, I think a Christian burial is what is rightfully deserved. No one's skull should be sitting around on display."

"It is hardly on display," Victoria pointed out. "Not when it's hidden away in an attic."

"Which raises an entirely new question," Bainbridge said. "Now, I can understand why initially the skull would have been hidden in the attic, back when the Royalists were still active, and there was a possibility the skull might be taken back and put on a pike yet again. But those days are long gone. So why was it still hidden? Why had it not been brought out, and claimed as the head of Oliver Cromwell? The other skull that is allegedly that of Cromwell has been brought to the public attention. So why not this one? Even if the Dunbars did not care to sell it, it is strange they have not mentioned the skull before now, and instead have left it to be discovered by someone who is quite clearly not really up to such a thing as determining its future."

"People do odd things," Victoria said. "Perhaps they thought something bad might happen if they tried to bury it. Someone might dig it up, so they could sell it on."

"Then the logical solution would be to bury it in secret," Bainbridge countered. "But that was not done either. All in all, it is very peculiar."

"At least we don't have the box sitting here before us anymore," Victoria groaned.

It had been left downstairs on the dining room table.

"I fancy it will get up to no mischief down there," Bainbridge said cheerfully. "Unlike us, who have all these papers and documents to sort through."

He glanced at the book he was looking at. It was a volume from 1854, written by the late Mr Dunbar. It was a diary of sorts, but also contained lists of geological stones, and other interesting scientific facts that he had gathered over the course of that particular year. There was a full section on experiments he had done involving sediment, and how it could determine the age of something buried in the earth. At first glance, it did not seem to be relevant to the skull, but it was such a chaotic and esoteric little book, that Bainbridge felt it was dangerous to ignore the possibility that somewhere among the clutter there might be a hint about the skull. So he was reading it from cover to cover.

Victoria was going through some old letters that had been written by a female member of the family back in the 1760s. At the moment, they did not seem to be revealing anything significant, other than that she had quite a fetish for ornate lace.

"We could be here days looking through all this," she said despondently.

"It hardly matters as long as Mr Dunbar is prepared to pay us for our time," Bainbridge pointed out.

"I suppose," Victoria said. "It is just, it seems less of a detective mystery then an active case. You know, where we are trying to help someone who is living and breathing, or trying to solve the mystery of the death of someone who was recently living and breathing."

"Do we decide who to help based on how long they have been dead or whether they are still alive?" Bainbridge questioned his niece.

"You are taking my words out of context," Victoria protested. "I admit, I struggle to sum up the feelings and emotions that are in my head just now. There is a part of me that feels this is a waste of time, that we could be dealing with a proper case, something that would benefit people who are still around."

"It is not as though we have another case to be working on that we have left behind to deal with this matter," Bainbridge reminded her.

"True," Victoria answered. "Maybe it is just that this skull worries me. I find it, well, creepy."

Bainbridge chuckled lightly.

"I think that it is safe to say that we all feel like that. Few people are quite happy to have a skull in their house, though I have encountered people who have a rather ghoulish sense of décor, and would gladly collect such peculiar items to furnish their rooms."

Victoria gave a small sigh and put down the letter she was looking at.

"I do not believe that Miss Beatrice Dunbar had any interest in this skull, or even knew about it. From reading her letters, and I hesitate to say this as it reflects poorly on the feminine sex, I believe she was something of a flighty girl. Her concerns were deeply shallow."

"Ah, but not all girls can be like you," Bainbridge said to her warmly. "You are exceptional, Victoria, and that is why I know you will help me with this case and we will find a satisfactory conclusion."

Despite herself, Victoria was flattered. It was not often her uncle praised her, or her abilities as a private detective. For a time, he hadn't even wanted her to be his assistant. Now she felt cheered by his praise, and continued with her work.

They had been going through the papers for nearly three hours when something caught Bainbridge's attention. It was an old inventory of the house conducted in 1671. If the skull was brought to the house after Cromwell's posthumous execution, it would have been around that time.

Oliver Cromwell died in 1658, from complications of malaria and a kidney stone. His body was exhumed in 1661. The inventory had been conducted just ten years after his skull had been removed from the pike and hidden somewhere.

Bainbridge was pleased to see that whoever had conducted the inventory had been very thorough. They had gone through all the floors of the house, including the attic, listing everything they saw. He started with the attic list, and was soon absorbed in reading about old crockery sets and ancient silverware. Some of the things documented, if they still remained in the attic, would be worth a small fortune today.

He scanned through the list, looking for what he wanted. He did not need to see that it listed a skull, he just needed to see that it mentioned a large lead box. If it did, then he could be quite sure that within it was the skull at that time, and it would mean that there was a close link between Oliver Cromwell and this house. It was not enough to say the skull was that of Oliver Cromwell, but it was certainly something that brought them closer to the truth.

But despite reading the inventory carefully, going through it twice, just to be sure, he found no mention of a lead box. He found plenty of mentions of other sorts of boxes, from ones that contained jewellery to some that contained tea. He found them listed as being made of rosewood, and silver, and one in gilt. But there was no mention of a lead box, and certainly not in the attic. This troubled him, especially as the inventory had been conducted by someone who was extremely efficient in their work, and had noted the smallest details. For example, the writer had taken the time to note that upon one shelf in the drawing room there were three loose nails. These were, of course, of no value, but the person who took the inventory clearly was serious about their work, and intended to record everything accurately.

Such a person would not miss a large lead box. This led Bainbridge to conclude that the box was not in the house at the time the inventory was made. What did that precisely mean? He scratched his chin and pondered.

What he could really do with was finding out how the officially identified Oliver Cromwell skull had been proven to be just that. If he could determine the means by which that had been identified, it might help him understand how he needed to identify this skull.

Equally, it could be of no use at all, he supposed.

"Julius," Victoria said suddenly. "You need to look at this."

Bainbridge looked up from his disappointing document.

"What is it?"

"I am reading through this booklet about the history of the family and the estate. It was written by one of the Dunbars, and it records that somewhere on the grounds there is an old family tomb. It had been in use since about 1617, when the earliest Dunbar came to this place, and decided that rather than being buried in the local graveyard, he wanted to be buried on his grounds. The family vault, as it might be termed, was then expanded, and contained several members of the family before it was finally sealed around 1700. It was set among some of the copses that are on this estate, and was partly below ground, so it would seem reasonable that very rapidly it would become overgrown, and covered with plants if left neglected. At the time the pamphlet was written, the location of the vault had been completely lost."

"So what are you thinking?" Bainbridge asked her.

"I am thinking that if you were going to randomly get a skull, you would go to an old family vault where you could obtain one easily."

"Who would desire to randomly acquire a skull?"

"Someone who perhaps wanted to claim they had the head of Oliver Cromwell," Victoria suggested. "Perhaps we are looking at all this the wrong way. Maybe it isn't about protecting the skull, rather it's about someone creating a hoax. People do things like that. Maybe they wanted to claim they had the original head so they could sell it one day. And then, of course, the actual head of Oliver Cromwell was discovered and sold on, so their plot was foiled."

"It is a sort of theory," Bainbridge concurred. "But we have no proof of it."

"I think we should go to this vault and look in it, and see if anybody is missing their head," Victoria said firmly.

Bainbridge had a slight smile on his face.

"I was not expecting such a remark from you," he declared. "Your general aversion to corpses, especially those of the long dead, causes me to have some surprise that you would be willing to go into a vault."

"It is all for the sake of this case," Victoria remarked. "Well, do you agree?"

"I agree that is as good a place as any to start looking," Bainbridge concurred. "After all, we have nothing else to go upon, and this inventory from 1671 does not list a lead box with or without a skull. Which makes me concerned that the skull was not here at that point. What that means I really can't say."

"What do you suppose Mr Dunbar will make of having a family vault in his grounds?" Victoria asked, ever so slightly smirking at the thought.

Bainbridge shook his head at her.

"I know what you are thinking, and it is rather mean. The poor man has already suffered enough. We shall not inflict the knowledge of a family tomb in his grounds upon him. We should go looking for it ourselves. Is there anything in that booklet that suggests where it might have been?"

"Not particularly. It must be somewhere there are lots of trees and overgrowth. We should be sure to find it if we go exploring and it is quite a lovely day."

They both glanced out of the window. It *was* a lovely day to go looking for a vault.

"Let us get to it then," Bainbridge said. "I, for one, could do with stretching my legs."

Chapter Seven

They went out into the grounds of the estate. Once the property had considerable gardens around the old house, but over the years portions had been sold off to raise funds for the family building projects. Expanding and improving the old house had been the priority of the family, and they had been happy to sell off distant areas of the gardens and grounds to neighbouring properties if it meant they could add a new wing or two. The grounds were still vast and required more than one gardener to keep on top of them. Looking further at the estate, Bainbridge mused that this was a place that cost a lot of money to run, and Mr Dunbar perhaps did not have a full appreciation of just how much it would cost him to be able to live here long term, at least to live here and ensure that everything stayed well maintained. Estates like this needed a very good income, and as far as he could tell, Mr Dunbar had none. He was going to rely on whatever he had received from his aunt. Still, that was not Bainbridge's problem. As long as he and Victoria got paid for what they were about to do, then anything else did not bother him.

He supposed for a moment that if the skull did prove to be that of Oliver Cromwell, it could be quite a coup for the family. Mr Dunbar could sell it for a lot of money if he could find a way around the clauses of his aunt's will. It would certainly raise some nice funds to keep the estate going, at least temporarily.

Victoria had been surveying the grounds; they led out into gardens and then turned into a series of small copses. You could not quite term them woods or forests, but they certainly were pretty little stands of trees. Many of them were quite overgrown with brambles and bracken and were happy haunts for rabbits, owls, rats, and the occasional bat. These were an area of the grounds that could be left untended and allowed to do as nature pleased.

Bainbridge took note of various groupings of trees, mostly beech, some sycamore, a few very old oaks. He baulked at the number of places they would have to search to look for the old family vault and felt a fraction daunted by it all. At least the sun was warming them, and there were quite a few hours of daylight still before the evening gently pulled in. In fact, it would probably be quite pleasant among the trees, as the sun still had some power to it, and Bainbridge was feeling a little flustered already. He did not do a great deal of exercise, and the walk from the house to the end of the grounds had taken it out of him. He pointed his walking stick towards a random copse.

"Shall we start there?"

Victoria followed his pointing stick. All she saw was a stand of sycamores, a few beeches, and lots of bushes tangled among them. The brambles were starting to flower and grow blackberries.

"Might as well," she said, thinking how her skirts were liable to get tangled among all those thorns. Still, that was the peril of being a private detective, and Victoria was getting quite good at making hidden repairs to her outfits. It had been quite some time since she had been able to afford a new dress and so she had to make sure her old ones were always serviceable.

"You lead the way, my dear," Bainbridge said confidently.

Victoria gave him a look, then headed towards the trees, supposing it was *her* idea to go looking for this legendary family vault. They were soon among the brambles, pushing them back as best they could and looking for anything that might indicate there was something underground.

"Do you have any idea what a family vault might look like?" Victoria asked her uncle as they moved through the trees.

She had snagged her hat on a tree branch and was trying to retrieve it.

"I presume it looks much like any sort of vault you find in a graveyard," Bainbridge responded. "Stone built. If it's underground, there will be stairs leading down to it, probably a door. The top is likely to be flat."

Thinking of this, he tapped his stick on the ground, hoping to hear something hard beneath it, such as the ring of stone. All that happened was that his stick poked into the dirt and stuck there for a second.

"This ground certainly retains water well," he observed, pulling out the stick.

"You would have thought someone would have left a map or something to tell us where the vault was," Victoria said resigning herself to tugging the hat out of the branches and hearing it rip.

"People do not always think like that," Bainbridge said. "They assume that because they know where a place is, everybody will know where it is. I can think of lots of places that just disappear with no trace."

"It all seems rather disorganised to me," Victoria said, annoyed he had challenged her observation. "Anyway, I suppose we best keep looking."

They wandered around through the trees for quite some time. For a while they were going in circles without realising it, and it wasn't until they came back to the spot where Victoria had lost her hat, that they discovered they had been going around and around. Groaning at their lack of direction, they moved off towards the far side of the trees, hoping they would finally take themselves out of their unconscious orbit. The trees thinned out and led to an area of open grass that was studded with small flowers. A neglected bench sat to one side. It was mostly rotten, and the seat had partly fallen through, but there was just a small enough piece for Bainbridge to perch on and rest his aching hips.

"Walking doesn't get any easier," he said, leaning hard on his stick and trying to stretch his back.

Victoria said nothing. They had had a discussion about his waistline, and whether losing some weight might actually aid his aches and pains. This had gone down like a lead canary. Bainbridge appreciated food, and nothing was going to stop him from continuing to appreciate it. He firmly believed it had nothing to do with his waistline that his hips and his knees ached. He felt it was due instead to some change in the world around him. He was convinced the ground had gotten harder for a start, and maybe the air heavier. Something like that. Something he could not control and just had to accept.

Seeing as he was not going to change, Victoria had stopped nagging him on the subject. Her early endeavours to tempt him with fresh fruit had been utter failures; his horrified look when she suggested he could eat tomatoes raw had been something to behold. Now she consoled herself as long as he ate at least one sort of vegetable a day. Preferably not cooked to mush, as Mrs Huggins enjoyed doing.

She studied the clearing and looked towards the trees, tilting her head and narrowing her eyes, she thought she saw something.

"Julius, do you not find it curious that there is a bench suddenly here among the trees?"

Bainbridge glanced in her direction.

"I had not given it a great deal of thought," he admitted. "I was thinking how convenient it was that someone had realised how far away these particular trees were from the house, and had placed a bench so you could stop and rest yourself. I felt it signified great forethought on the part of whoever put this bench here."

"I was thinking that it indicated there was a reason for it being here, perhaps because people came this direction a lot, and might want to sit and muse on things," Victoria suggested. "Such as musing about a relative who had recently passed and was buried in a vault nearby?"

Bainbridge saw where she was going with this. He tapped the bench. It was old, very old. He could suppose it had been around since the 1600s. Its decayed state indicated that it had long ago become neglected. Once it had been heavily stained with preservative to keep it from rotting away. Now the rain had seeped into it, the insects had burrowed through it, and it was slowly, slowly disintegrating.

"If you are correct," Bainbridge said. "Where do you suppose this tomb is?"

Victoria pointed in the direction of the trees before her.

"I think I can see something through those trees, something perpendicular. It might just be another tree trunk, but supposing it is an upright piece of stone, such as that which would line the front of a vault."

"It sounds like a wonderful thing to investigate," Bainbridge concluded. "I shall let you do that since it is your idea."

This meant he was not getting off the bench unless there was something he really needed to look at. Giving a small huff, Victoria walked into the trees, and went about the same complicated business of trying to avoid snagging her clothes on the brambles and branches. She was starting to think there must be a better outfit for traipsing through woods, when she nearly tripped over something on the ground. She thought it was a tree root at first, but when she noted the throbbing in her toe from where she had stubbed it, she decided that it might have been something harder. She scraped about in the dirt, trying not to think about how filthy her hands were now getting, and found that she was looking at a small lump of stone. It was not an ordinary rock that you might just find on the ground, it had been shaped into a rectangle, such as a brick might be shaped. She studied it for a moment, then stood and looked around her. The stone could not be far from wherever the vault was, she theorised, unless there was some other feature that had once been in the grounds and had now been forgotten. The trees seem very dense around here, and there was an extremely large holly bush. She stared and stared at the holly bush, something about it causing her to be curious. Then she stepped forward and, with care because the holly was spiky, she put her hands through the leaves and felt around.

Her guess was rewarded by her discovering a solid surface beyond. It was cold and smooth, and felt like stone. This had to be the vault or what remained of it. It was not far above the ground, she noted. Only coming to just above her waist height, which meant the rest was probably underground. There had to be a set of stairs going down to it, but where? She could have really done with Bainbridge's stick at this point to fudge around in the ground, but since he was not present, she very daintily felt around with her foot to see if beneath the floor of thick brambles, and other vegetation, there might be a space. She could not find one here, but it had to be close, so she carefully followed the edge of the vault and turned to her left.

Even being extremely careful, she nearly fell headfirst into a dip in the ground, which proved to be an old flight of stairs leading downwards. Her foot had simply gone away from under her, and it had only been by a sheer fluke of luck that she had managed to grab hold of something in the holly and had saved herself. That *something* proved to be an ornamental acorn-shaped device that had been sitting on the front of the tomb, like a pedestal. She clung to this and pulled herself back out of the hole. Then she stared downwards.

"Well, I found the steps," she said to herself.

Victoria became conscious that she was speaking to no one.

"This is what comes with being too long alone with Uncle Julius," she complained to herself, before noting she was doing it again.

She recovered her composure and headed back towards the clearing.

"Julius, I have located the vault," she told her uncle proudly.

He had been resting in a relaxed manner, his head placed upon his hands which were atop his stick. He had closed his eyes and in this position seemed to be dozing off. It was remarkable just how Bainbridge could doze off in any particular stance, given the right circumstances.

He opened his eyes sharply, and became alert again.

"You have found it, really?"

"You could try to look less surprised," Victoria scolded him. "After all, it was my idea, and I am not that bad a detective."

"That wasn't what I meant," Bainbridge said apologetically. "I was just surprised there actually was a vault. I was starting to think it was some sort of family legend."

"There is definitely something in those woods. I nearly fell down the steps leading to whatever it is. Come look for yourself."

Bainbridge levered himself off the bench and followed her, looking a bit stiff as he came. Victoria almost said something about him needing to get into better condition when she saw how he hobbled, but decided it was not worth the argument that would follow. Bainbridge considered the cure for most things was a good slice of cake and a cup of tea. How could she possibly persuade him that stopping such comforts would improve his health?

They headed through the undergrowth, and she showed him where she had located the opening in the ground. He poked around with his stick and swept away some old leaves revealing a staircase. It was narrow and it went down between two brick lined walls that marked the sides of the deep hole. They couldn't see what was at the base of the steps because trailing ivy had covered nearly everything beyond the stairs, but it was safe to assume that there was a doorway.

"I do declare you have done it, Vicky," Bainbridge smiled at her. "We have found the long lost Dunbar family vault."

Chapter Eight

"Family vaults," Victoria said with an uneasy edge to her voice. "It all seems slightly, I don't know…"

"Morbid," Bainbridge suggested. "Creepy? Unsavoury?"

"Claustrophobic," Victoria finally found the word she wanted. "That is what it feels like. Claustrophobic. I mean, you spend all your life with your family. Do you really want to spend your eternity buried with them?"

"Depending on your religious outlook," Bainbridge said, "you would not expect to spend eternity with them, at least not buried in a vault together. But I do get your point. I suppose it all depends on how you sit within your family. Some people take these things very seriously."

Victoria shot a look at him.

"Would you care to have your corpse buried alongside my mother's corpse forever?"

"I will admit that does not tickle my fancy," Bainbridge confessed. "As much as I love my sister, she is, shall we say, difficult?"

"That is putting it mildly," Victoria remarked, a smile creeping onto her lips. "But there you go. I suppose some people are taken by these sort of things. Some people feel it is right and proper to have all their family around them."

"Some people like the idea of keeping everybody close," Bainbridge said. "Personally, I wouldn't care if my grave was somewhere in the middle of a forest, unidentified by any marker or gravestone, and completely forgotten about. I do not need people coming to mourn over me."

Victoria considered this.

"Surely if you were buried in the middle of a forest, it would suggest that you might have been murdered and secretly hidden there, especially if your burial place was forgotten?"

Bainbridge was amused by this remark.

"In my line of work it is quite the possibility. In fact, it sounds rather interesting."

Victoria was not sure whether to take that as humour, all be it 'Bainbridge humour', or to assume he was serious. In any case, it was time to stop dithering on the doorstep, and to get down into the tomb. The corpses were not going to get any less dead the longer they waited around outside.

They found that the vault was sealed with a wooden door for ease of access, in front of this was a wrought iron gate. The gate had at one time been locked, but years of being out in the elements had caused the chain that secured it, and the old padlock, to rust away. It only took a few good strikes with a heavy stone and the whole thing fell off. The iron gate creaked and groaned as they wedged it open; the hinges were so rusty they could only pry it out by a few inches.

Bainbridge looked at the tight gap despondently.

"I shall not fit through there," he said, rubbing his belly in a sad fashion; it was not often that Bainbridge regretted his girth, but sometimes he did feel it was a hindrance.

Victoria also looked at the narrow gap. She could fit through it, but did she really want to be in a vault with mouldering corpses all alone? With grim determination, she decided that the gate would be forced to open fully. It took some doing, some hefting and heaving, and pushing back and forth, and it probably wouldn't have worked at all except one of the hinges actually snapped through, but with a good deal of effort – that was perhaps not terribly ladylike in fashion and resulted in Victoria huffing, and puffing, and sweating – the gate finally was wrenched open to a suitable width to allow Bainbridge to go through.

The wooden door beyond was less of a problem. It had only been intended to mask the inside of the vault and never to be a particular deterrent to...

Well, who exactly did you deter from vaults in the English countryside? Graverobbers? It was hardly ancient Egypt where tombs were filled with glorious treasures, and graverobbers might be expected to go down and steal everything in sight.

Still, Victoria supposed it kept the foxes and other animals out, to a degree. There were bound to be gaps and holes where the smallest of creatures could find their way through. They barely touched the wooden door and it started to crumble before them. The handle simply fell off. The door opened inwards, bits and pieces from the top and bottom falling onto the earth. Beyond was a gaping black hole. They could smell the dust of ages. Dust that had probably not seen the light of day since the final family member had been buried there.

Victoria was starting to lose her nerve again. She glanced at her uncle.

"This seemed a marvellous idea when we were back in the library," she said uncomfortably. "Now I am here, I am not convinced it was quite the right one."

"It is a very logical idea," Bainbridge consoled her. "There is a family vault in the grounds, and there's a mysterious head in the house – the two things rather go together."

"Yes, that makes sense, and in that regard the notion is perfectly reasonable," Victoria admitted. "However, I do not think I really considered quite what it would be like to actually go into the vault."

"You have become a lot braver these days around bodies," Bainbridge told her proudly. "This should be no obstacle for you."

Victoria was consoled by his praise. She glanced again into the murky gloom which was gradually beginning to take shape before her. She could see coffins stacked one upon another.

"How precisely do you propose we go about all this?" She said to her uncle, giving a small shudder. "Are we going to have to open those coffins?"

"I am afraid that will be the case," Bainbridge replied, and Victoria was sure there was a slight cheerfulness in his tone. "We must check that every single body has its head. And if they do, well, that is one line of investigation we can discard."

Victoria glanced into the murk. She took a deep breath. As much as she hated the notion of having to step into the vault, she really felt she ought to go first. She had nearly allowed her unease to get the better of her, and she wasn't going to allow that to happen again. She wanted to prove herself as a detective and, should she add, as a woman. So many men assumed women were these flighty, screaming things that could not keep their heads in an emergency. She was determined to prove that was completely wrong, and she was not going to do that if every time they came across a tomb or vault, or some similar scenario, she began to feel queasy and had to retreat. She told herself firmly she was not going to faint.

She was unaware that her uncle was watching her, studying the motion on her face as her expression changed, and almost reading her thoughts. He was deeply proud of how his niece had developed over the last few months. How she was coming into her own, becoming braver, overcoming her fears. He deliberately held back, even though he was itching to get into the tomb. He would have gladly gone in first, and searched all the coffins by himself, but he knew that this was a moment when Victoria needed to take charge. It had been her idea, and she needed to overcome her fear of the dead.

Victoria walked into the tomb. She held her breath as she entered, not wanting to taste the stale air of centuries ago. She had to close her eyes for a second as she entered. Then she stood in the midst of it the tomb. It was not big, just wide enough so that the coffins could be laid out on either side, and stacked three deep, with a narrow corridor between them. As she stood in the middle, she could sense the presence of the wooden coffins on either side of her.

It was bad enough, she told herself, to look upon them, let alone to be stood there, knowing they were beside her, with her eyes shut. She opened her eyes and faced her fear. Of course, the coffins were closed at this moment in time, and all she saw was a lot of rotting wood. Bainbridge shuffled in behind her. He discovered that the passage between the sets of coffins was not all that wide and he had to take a deep breath to get himself between them.

"I wonder if they stacked them chronologically," he said, tapping his bottom lip. He peered at one of the coffins. "It's no good, Vicky. We are going to need a lamp of some description."

"We ought to have considered that," Victoria said with regret. "We came out rather unprepared for vault exploring."

Bainbridge smiled at her.

"I think we can resolve the problem fairly easily," he said. "It appears that in the past, someone anticipated coming down to this vault and sitting with their late family members. You can tell that because they had lamps installed. Look at each corner."

Victoria looked where he pointed, and there, in sconces on the wall, were two old lamps. They were a primitive sort which could have been filled with oil to burn or candles could have been stood in them.

"It may even be they were installed to enable those who brought the coffins down here to see better," Bainbridge added. "I wonder if any of them still have a little bit of fuel sitting in their bases. Oil doesn't really go anywhere, after all."

He reached out to the nearest one and dipped his finger carefully over the edge. It came back slightly sticky.

"Well, yes, there do appear to be some remnants of oil. It seems whoever had this vault made, decided oil lamps were advisable and created them in the old style of the Romans. Quite logical really. Oil burns a little cleaner than a grubby tallow candle."

Victoria wondered where he was headed. It might be that ancient oil was sitting in the lamp holders, but how did that help them?

"We have no matches," she told her uncle.

Bainbridge grinned. He rooted in a pocket and produced a box of matches.

"I always carry them, as you never know when you might need them," he said.

They were safety matches and he struck them carefully along the side of the box, then held one towards the old oil. It didn't immediately light. It was covered with debris, spider webs, and dust. It took a while for everything to burn through and for the oil to touch the flame. Then it quickly took and a faint glow spread across the top of the oil lamp.

The single lamp did not cast off a great deal of light, but there were three more of them – one in each corner – they lit them all and in the dim glow that the lamps produced, they were able finally to see the coffins.

"Considering the nature of this vault, I have to say the coffins these people would put in are rather crude," Bainbridge said, looking at the rough wood before him. There was a name plate on the coffin nearest him, and he rubbed at it with a finger.

"Prudence Dunbar," he read out. "She perished in the year 1699. Well, let's see if she has her head."

Despite the slightly rough nature of the coffins, they were firmly nailed together. Bainbridge had to get his stick and wedge its handle under one end to try and pull away the lid. Fortunately, the tomb was rather damp, and the wood had become saturated with moisture over the years. It was completely rotten and it creaked open easier than expected. With a flurry of dust, they revealed the corpse of Prudence Dunbar. There was not a great deal to see. She had been laid to rest in a fine dress, which was now almost disintegrated to nothing, but you could still make out that it had been trimmed with lace. It had probably been finely embroidered. Her corpse itself was reduced to mere bones, and she had her head.

"Well, that solves that," Bainbridge said.

"How are we going to get beyond Prudence to the coffin below?" Victoria asked.

Bainbridge surveyed the coffins.

"There is only one option. We shall have to lift it off," he said. "And take it out into the sunlight. I don't suppose Prudence will mind."

Victoria pulled a face. Prudence might not mind, but she did. However, it did not seem they had an option, so she agreed. They had to search every coffin to rule out the possibility that a deceased Dunbar was the head in the box. Fortunately, neither coffin nor deceased weighed very much, and so between them it was relatively easy for them to take the coffin out, negotiate it up the steps and place it on the ground.

"I really hope Mr Dunbar does not come along and see all this," Victoria said, thinking how they were removing his ancestors from their tomb in a rather disrespectful fashion. "How on earth do we explain to him firstly that there is a family vault in his grounds, and secondly that we are looking for one that is lacking a head?"

"We would explain it carefully and slowly," Bainbridge told her. "That is always the best way."

Then they went back into the vault.

There were six coffins in total, including Prudence. There was no room for anymore, and presumably this had been the number intended from the start. Perhaps the people who were buried here had even selected their slot in this vault. Whatever the case, they worked through them all until they finally came to Mathias Dunbar – the person who had commissioned the family vault. He died in 1685 and it would seem logical that if anyone was to lose their skull, only for it to appear in the family attic, it would be his.

However, when they opened his coffin, there he was, his head intact.

There was only one slight problem.

Mathias Dunbar had his head, but he also had another sitting beside him.

A second disembodied skull very similar to the one in the mysterious box.

Chapter Nine

Victoria and Bainbridge stared into the coffin. For once, Victoria found herself speechless.

"This was not what I was expecting," Bainbridge said, staring in at the second skull. "I am quite confused by this."

"Confused?" Victoria asked. "That is all you are? Confused."

Bainbridge stared at the coffin.

"I will admit I am somewhat perplexed as well."

"Personally, I am horrified," Victoria said dryly. "No one ought to have a second skull in their coffin."

"I must admit that is very curious," Bainbridge confessed. He was tapping his finger on his chin again. "There has to be some meaning for this, some reason behind it."

"I am starting to wonder if the Dunbar family had a ghoulish obsession with collecting stray heads," Victoria remarked. "Where were they getting them from?"

Bainbridge had to admit that was a good question. You didn't just come across random loose heads. The real question, however, was what to do about it now they had found the second skull. Bainbridge felt it was logical that they should remove it and take it to the house, and perhaps put it with the other skull they had indoors to compare them.

Victoria was not so sure. When he suggested they remove this skull and take it up to the house, she baulked at the idea.

"I hardly think that is wise. It will upset Mr Dunbar," she said, really meaning it would upset her.

"In this instance, I don't think Mr Dunbar's feelings can be taken into account," Bainbridge explained. "There is some deeper mystery going on here, and we have to dig into it. If that means taking the skull back to the house, and possibly upsetting the poor fellow, well, we will just have to do it."

Victoria pulled a face. Her nose wrinkled up and she almost wished to sneer at the skull. Her disgust for this whole morbid adventure was very palatable.

"Maybe," Bainbridge paused. "Maybe this is actually the skull of a relative."

"You are being somewhat optimistic there," Victoria pointed out.

"Well, the vault is only so big. Supposing more people wanted to be buried in it than there was room for? Perhaps a compromise was to just bury their heads?"

"Did you actually hear what you just said?" Victoria asked him, horrified again at the notion.

"It was the sort of thing done quite commonly in the past."

"Which past are you referring to?" His niece glared at him.

Bainbridge hesitated. He was thinking of the ancient past, sometime, perhaps, in the Bronze Age when such practises were commoner.

"Very well, perhaps that isn't the answer. However, supposing the fellow was executed, and all they could get back was his head?"

"Julius, this is starting to get ridiculous," Victoria told him sternly. "Executed or not, people don't go around placing random heads in other people's coffins or keeping them in boxes in the house."

"In that regard, you do have a point," Bainbridge admitted. "But I stick by my words. We have to take this head back to the house. We need to work out what is going on here."

Victoria was not impressed, but she conceded his argument. They had to investigate this second skull, just as they had to investigate the first.

I suppose we must take it back to the house," she said. "I am not carrying it though."

"I never supposed you were going to carry it."

Her uncle gave her a smug look, which had the desired effect he had intended. Spurned by his look of satisfaction that he had predicated she would refuse to take the skull, she stepped forward, reached into the coffin, and lifted the entire horrible object out. She was grimacing as she did it, and she held it as far away from her as she could.

"We ought to find something to wrap it in," Bainbridge said casually.

Victoria cast him a hard glance, and he decided it was probably best not to carry on with his teasing. When she had that look on her face, she rather reminded him of his sister.

"Moving on," he said. "Shall we leave these coffins as they are? We could always round up a gardener and ask them to put them back."

Victoria, still with the skull held at arm's length away from her, looked at the coffins that they had heaved out of the vault and laid upon the ground outside. They had not arranged them terribly neatly, haste having been the order of the moment. She felt rather bad leaving them all scattered around. It rather felt like desecration.

Sighing to herself, she propped the skull neatly atop what remained of the vault and then she nodded to her uncle.

"We best put them all back while we can."

Bainbridge had rather hoped she would agree to the gardener idea; his back was starting to play up. Reluctantly, he helped her with the coffins. It took longer to take them back down the stairs than it had to bring them out in the first place. It was awkward, and more than once they slipped and the coffins fell to one side, or came close to falling to pieces in their hands. When they were done, Bainbridge was quite out of breath, and looked rather red in the face. It was not often that Victoria was truly concerned about her uncle's health, but in that moment she looked at him with concern.

"We should get back to the house," she told him. "But we will take it slowly."

Bainbridge made no protest. He did not have the breath in him to speak.

Collecting the skull, Victoria led the way back to the house. They took their time, and the sun had started to droop in the sky as they found themselves returning to the property.

Victoria had noted there was a slight aroma from what remained of the skull. It still had a fraction of hair attached to the scalp, and the remains of blackened skin. She had an unfortunate amount of time to study it, even though she had tried her hardest not lay her eyes upon it. She was becoming uncomfortably familiar with the skull, noticing its lines and features, finding her gaze drawn into the huge sockets that once contained eyeballs.

Despite herself, she found she was wondering who had possessed this skull in life. Did it belong to a man or woman? Had they been young, old, handsome, pretty, ugly? Had they been much loved, or had they been the sort of person nobody particularly cared about? Maybe they had been kind, maybe they hadn't. At the end of their days, all that remained was this; bone and scraps of skin. Nothing to say who this person had been or, what they had been like. She was not sure if that made her feel sad or whether it simply caused her to realise that whatever happened in this life, ultimately, they all came to the same fate. They all ended up like this – a skull that revealed nothing about its former owner. It did not say anything of their personality, who they had been, or the decisions they had made in life.

In a strange way that was almost comforting, or maybe it was just a case that Victoria was getting far too used to hanging around with dead bodies.

They reached the house and Bainbridge quickly found himself a chair to rest in. He looked more exhausted than was usual. Victoria carefully concealed the skull under a table, and then rang the bell to summon the grim-faced Mr Jennings. The butler arrived so swiftly, it appeared he must have been nearby. Victoria almost wondered if he had been watching them.

Jennings took one look at the exhausted Bainbridge and went straight into action.

"I believe tea is required," he said. "Possibly some small sandwiches? Something to restore the gentleman's energy and health."

"That sounds most agreeable," Bainbridge concurred.

At least the flushed colour in his face was diminishing.

When Jennings had departed, Victoria sat next to her uncle. She took his hand in hers.

"I overworked you today," she said sorrowfully.

"I overworked myself," Bainbridge told her, gently smiling. "I never can resist a good mystery. But do not fret, I shall be perfectly fine."

"At least you are still in good cheer," Victoria added, there was the vaguest hint of a tear in her eyes. She had really been quite concerned about her uncle as they had walked back. In the short time they had come to work together, she had grown deeply fond of him. She felt more connected to him than any other member of her family. She would hate anything to happen to him.

"I want to take another look at that skull," Bainbridge said, now starting to feel better.

Victoria fetched it from its hiding place and presented it to her uncle. He set it in his lap, and looked deeply into the eyes.

"Who were you?" He asked the skull.

"I am starting to wonder if we will ever be able to determine that," Victoria frowned. "We have no clue as to who this skull might have been, nor why his or her head turned up in someone else's coffin."

"I must admit this is a case where the clues are very limited," Bainbridge said. He was turning the head around and around in his hands. "I think our first task will be to examine the Dunbar family tree, to compare it with those family members we found in the vault, and to determine if someone is missing."

"You still think this might be the head of some old Dunbar? One who for some reason could not fit in their entirety in the actual tomb?"

"It does seem the most logical answer. Otherwise, we are faced with the possibility that one of the Dunbars rather liked taking peoples' heads off their necks."

Victoria shivered at that notion. Even though these people had been long dead, it was still rather awful to suppose what they might have been doing or had had done to them.

Jennings returned with the tea things. The sandwiches he had mentioned were very small and cut into slim rectangles. Bainbridge looked upon them with approval. For a moment, he did not even notice that the butler was staring at the skull in his lap.

The look on Jennings' face was best described as one of shock, though he was doing a good job of masking it. Butlers were trained not to show their emotions, even when peculiar things turned up in the house. Jennings was a professional and he was not going to demonstrate that he was disturbed at all by what was sitting in Bainbridge's lap.

"It is not the one from the box," Bainbridge told him when he spied his face. "We found this in a long lost family vault in the grounds. It was nestled alongside Mathias Dunbar, who happened to have his own head intact."

A slight twitch began around Jennings' left eye.

"More skulls, Sir?" He asked in a very matter of fact tone. He might have been simply asking whether they wanted more tea.

"Quite," Bainbridge said. "There are certainly a fair few mysteries about this property."

"It has been in the family many, many years," Jennings said noncommittally.

It was the most the butler had spoken to them. It appeared the sight of the skull had rather loosened his lips. He could not take his eyes off the thing.

"I know we asked you before Jennings," Victoria spoke. "But do you recall your mistress or your former master saying anything about these skulls? I don't suppose they ever asked you to do something hideous such as dust them, but they might have mentioned their existence."

"I fear on that front, I can offer you nothing," Jennings said firmly. "I was never privy to any information about these mysterious objects."

His tone suggested he was quite glad of that fact.

"Is there anything else?" He asked.

"No, you can go Jennings," Bainbridge assured him.

The butler was only too glad to leave the room and departed with unseemly haste.

"Well, I think we have shaken him up enough for today. I believe he knows nothing about these skulls."

Bainbridge placed the skull on a table before them. It was strange to have the eyeless head glaring at them. It seemed to want tell them something.

"I don't like this at all," Victoria said to her uncle. "I think something rather nasty has happened here."

"You may be right," her uncle replied. "But whatever this thing is, we are going to resolve it and bring Mr Dunbar peace of mind."

"I wish I had your confidence," Victoria said. "Or your clarity. I find myself wondering what could possibly have happened all those centuries ago. It gives me a shudder just to think about it."

"I would suggest not thinking about it is the best option."

"Try explaining that to him," Victoria pointed at the skull. "If it is a man. We don't know that, of course. Skulls look rather genderless."

"Death is the great unifier. We used to say that in the army," Bainbridge said. "In death we all the same."

"The difference," Victoria said bleakly, "is how we get there."

Bainbridge had to agree with her logic. They both found themselves sitting before the skull for at least an hour, lost in their own thoughts. Neither spoke or raised any questions. They were, in fact, still sitting in morbid reflection as the sun set outside, and the long evening shadows fell over them. Partly this was because Bainbridge had fallen asleep.

Victoria, however, was thinking hard about the case before them and what it could mean. No matter how she twisted and turned it in her head, she couldn't come up with an answer that seemed reasonable. It wasn't just that they had no idea who the head belonged to, it was also the fact that someone had bothered to place it in the coffin of old Mathias Dunbar, and presumably that same person had also placed the skull in the lead box in the attic. Was that significant?

It was simply too many questions and not enough answers.

When the bell rang out in the house to summon them to dinner, Victoria took the skull from the table, carried it through the house, and placed it beside the other skull they had discovered. She looked at the pair for a while, wondering what to do next. Then she went around the room and locked the two doors that opened into the room.

She took the keys with her, safe in the knowledge that both skulls were now trapped inside the room. They would not be accidentally stumbled upon by a hapless servant. Mr Dunbar did not need the maids being upset after all. Then she tried as much as she could to put the skulls out of her mind.

She did not think she was going to sleep very well that night.

Chapter Ten

B ainbridge had an uncomfortable night.

He assumed it was the after effects of too much exercise, but as the night waned on, and he noticed a peculiar sensation in his chest, he started to worry. After trying to fall asleep with the tightness crossing his breast, he determined that nothing was going to help him save getting up and carrying on with the mystery. There was no point lying in bed worrying about what might be.

He rose, pretended there was nothing wrong, and headed to the family library. All was quiet.

He found a candle and lit it, then went to the bookshelf that contained the family papers. He cast his eye along the many books and documents, and finally saw something that intrigued him. It was the family Bible. A great, bulky tome that dominated the shelves and barely fit in the space it had been allotted. Family Bibles typically contained a family tree at the beginning. Bainbridge removed the book, which was heavy and sizeable, and placed it with a slight thud on the table. He noted that the pain in his chest was still there. He rubbed at his breast bone.

A cloud of dust had risen when he had dropped the book on the table, indicating the Bible had not been off the shelf in quite some time. He opened its front cover, noting the appearance of silverfish in the book, which indicated the whole library was probably affected. He rubbed his hand across the first page, brushing away small flecks of dirt and debris that had collected in the tome over the years.

Turning over the first leaf, he found exactly what he had hoped for – a detailed family tree. It stretched back to the purchase of the Bible, which he was delighted to see had been in 1635. He glanced through the antique handwriting and spotted Mathias, then he scrolled his finger down to study the names of the other family members.

What he really needed to do was work out who was missing, *if* there was anyone missing, from the vault. He knew the rough dates that the tomb had been in use, therefore, he could compare the names from the coffins in the vault with the family tree for that period, and determine who might have found themselves without room for their whole body inside the family mausoleum.

He considered this statement for a second. How many people thought to themselves, 'well, if I cannot fit my whole body into the vault, I shall just have my head buried there.' Though, considering what they had so far discovered on the Dunbar property, if any family was to be of such a disposition, it would be them.

He determined not to dwell on it. Instead, he went around the library and found some paper, a pen and ink. He then settled himself to copying the names. The handwriting was old and the ink had faded to a brown rust colour. He had to carefully read each one because the script was not easy to follow. He slowly unravelled the names. Mathias Dunbar, the originator of the tomb, had had a brother. This gentleman had passed away before Matthias, despite being the younger sibling, and ought to be in the vault.

It was then Bainbridge realised he could not recall all the names he had read on the coffins earlier. He cursed himself for neglecting to write down the names, an oversight that had been brought on by him feeling unwell.

Normally, Bainbridge was not so careless. In any case, he would have to go back and note the names on the coffins to compare against this list.

He carried on.

Matthias was married and had two daughters and a son. One of these was Prudence, who never married. He recalled her coffin was the first they had opened. The second daughter was named Rosa, and she married a gentleman who went by the name of Jennings. Bainbridge paused at the curious coincidence. How odd he thought; then again, Jennings was not an uncommon name.

Matthias' son was named Oliver, and Bainbridge smiled at the connection to the famous Cromwell. Looking at the dates that the child was born, it would have been right around the English Civil War. Would it be so farfetched to assume he had been named in homage to the great Lord Protector?

Oliver had married and had three sons of his own. Bainbridge took down the names and made a quick count in his head. He had Mathias in the vault, potentially his brother and, logically, there would be Mathias' wife, who was named Anna. Next, he had Prudence, who he knew had been buried in the family vault, which brought the total to four. Finally, there was Mathias' son, and perhaps his son's wife, which would bring the total to six. Assuming that the daughter, Rosa, had not opted to be buried in the family vault, as she would surely have been laid to rest wherever her husband's family were buried. She probably had moved away after her marriage, in any case.

That left the three sons of Oliver. Would they have wanted to be buried in the family vault? The number of potential people in the vault had already reached six, which was the number of coffins Bainbridge had seen. He glanced again at the names.

Assuming Matthias had planned for the vault to house him, and his immediate family, he had underestimated the size it needed to be. He had made it too small. After all, once he had taken into account his brother, himself, his wife and two of his children, along with his son's spouse, there had been no room for anybody else.

Bainbridge briefly considered going back to the vault right then to take a look at the coffins. He raised his head and looked out the windows across the grounds, which were shrouded in the shadows of night. He shook his head. No, that was ridiculous. After all the exertion of the afternoon, he really needed to be more sensible. He rubbed absently at his chest, and then realised that the tightness had gone. Relieved by this, he blew out his candle, closed the Bible and started back towards his bedroom.

He was halfway across the landing, when he heard a strange noise. Down below, he thought he heard a shuffling, followed by something that was a muffled bang. He paused. He was completely in the dark. There were no windows at this section of the house to light the landing, and he was relying on what little light came from downstairs. The noise was distinctive. The more he listened, the more he was sure someone was moving about in the dark.

Bainbridge had never been a person to shirk away from his duty, and now he heard the noise, he knew he needed to ascertain whether there were housebreakers entering the property. He considered for only a minute more, and then headed down the stairs as quietly as he could. Despite his size, Bainbridge was surprisingly nimble, and he could move as quietly as a mouse when he wished.

He reached the front hall and paused to listen again. The noise was soft and difficult to make out, but he was certain now there was someone moving around in one of the rooms. As he traced the sound further into the house, he realised, somewhat alarmingly, the noise was coming from the old dining room where they had left the skulls.

The house was big enough to support two dining rooms. They were referred to as the old and the new one. The previous night they had dined in the new one, which Mr Dunbar favoured. It was furnished in a relatively modern style compared to the old one, which had not been updated in several centuries. His aunt had preferred the old one, with its rustic worn table that had seen many family dinners over the years. Mr Dunbar did not suffer from the same sentimentality, understandably, as his connection to the family was only recent, and he preferred the airiness of the newer dining room.

Unknown to Bainbridge, Victoria had locked all the doors to the old dining room. He now headed towards the room, and as he listened, he was sure he heard someone moving about inside.

He noted there was no sign of a light coming through from under the doors, so no one had lit the gas or was carrying a candle. Suspicious indeed. He went to the door and tried the handle. It did not move. The door was still locked.

His efforts, however, had alerted the person within the room and, suddenly, everything went quiet.

"Whoever is in there, I intend to lay hands on you," Bainbridge told them through the door. "I won't have house breaking when I am around."

He hoped he sounded very belligerent and confident. He wasn't feeling either of those things at that moment. He was stood in his dressing gown and slippers, still feeling slightly dazed from his earlier exertions, and still worrying about the pain that had been in his chest, which he was now endeavouring to convince himself was just indigestion.

"Give it up!" he declared. "You cannot get away. The door is locked."

After he said this, it occurred to Bainbridge that since he had not locked the door, perhaps the person who was in the room had, which rather negated his warning.

Beyond the door, everything had fallen deadly silent. Bainbridge rattled the handle again, but it was no use. The door was firmly locked. He remembered there was a second door into the room, though he could not for the life of him quite recall how he reached it, as it was not near this door. He headed off in exploration, determined to get into the room and locate the suspect. He was listening all the time for movement from the dining room. He found his way to the second door; it was down a side corridor, and linked to another drawing room. He tried the door and found it was also locked.

"The fellow has the key," he said to himself angrily.

He rattled the doors violently. Well, as violently as Bainbridge ever did anything.

"Excuse me, Sir."

Bainbridge nearly jumped out of his skin at the voice behind him. He spun around and saw that Jennings had appeared. He was also in his dressing gown and slippers, and carrying a candle. He looked quite dignified in his nightwear. In contrast to Bainbridge, who tended to look a little bit ruffled whenever he was in his dressing gown. It didn't help that the dressing gown only just covered his belly these days.

"Jennings, you gave me a start."

"I do apologise Sir, but I heard someone moving around, and I thought I had better come and investigate."

It was a very reasonable statement.

"I am sure someone is in the old dining room," Bainbridge told him. "I heard them moving about when I was upstairs."

Jennings gave him a look; it should have been impossible for Bainbridge to have heard sounds from the dining room while in his bedroom, which was at the back of the house. Bainbridge felt that an explanation was necessary.

"I just thought I would take a little stroll around the house," he said, only remembering later that it was completely unnecessary to explain himself to a butler.

Jennings merely nodded.

"I am sorry to hear you were feeling unwell, Sir. If there is anything I can do..."

Bainbridge did not let him finish his statement.

"What is more important is getting into that room, and finding out who has broken into the house. They could be stealing everything."

Jennings cast an eye towards the doors.

"There is nothing of great value in the dining room," he remarked. "It is rather barren of antiques and other such items. They must be attempting to use it as a way to gain access to the rest of the house."

"Well, that is likely the case," Bainbridge agreed. "But still, we need to get in. It has gone awfully quiet."

"You will find, Sir, the doors are not locked," Jennings said to him.

Bainbridge shook his head.

"But they are locked. I checked."

Jennings had a confused look on his face. He headed to the door and tried it for himself. Frowning, he felt in his pocket for a ring of keys that he carried. Among them was the spare key to the dining room. He fitted the key in the lock, turned it, and the doors obediently swung open. They stepped into the room. It was thick with shadows. Jennings automatically went to the wall fittings, turned on the gas, and used his candle to light them. It took a moment for him to light all the relevant sconces, but slowly the room came into focus.

Bainbridge was looking around quickly, trying to see if there was any place a burglar could hide. The room was quite barren when it came to furniture. There were no cupboards or handy corners that someone could sneak into. He also noted that the windows were shut. He walked over to the nearest one and tried it. It opened easily.

"They could have come in through a window," he said, testing it again.

"I must admit, Sir, they are not the most secure of windows," Jennings remarked. "I mentioned it to Mr Dunbar, I had mentioned it also to his late aunt, as I felt they were a vulnerability."

Bainbridge said no more. He allowed the window to slip fully shut. Yes, he could see how someone could have climbed through it and, once outside, pushed it closed, to make it appear as if the window had been shut all the time.

"Well, that tells us how they got in," he sighed. "And it looks like they have vanished without a trace."

"You must have disturbed them, Sir," Jennings said calmly. "What a good thing you were overhead when they were moving around."

There seemed a hint of sarcasm in Jennings' voice, but Bainbridge told himself he was probably imagining it. It was then his eyes went to the large table. Until that point he had not looked at it because he had been so busy scanning the room for places the burglar could hide. Now he noticed that it was empty.

He froze.

It was empty!

"Jennings," he cried in alarm. "Someone has nicked the skulls."

Chapter Eleven

Victoria had been deep in a dream when there was a pounding on her bedroom door. She started awake, and for a moment she was in that hazy place between sleep and alertness, where she wondered if the knocking had been part of her dream or was real. The knocking had stopped briefly, then it started again, and she realised someone really was trying to wake her.

She sat up in bed, drew on her slippers, pulled the dressing gown around her shoulders, and headed to the door. She was naturally anxious to find out what was going on. She assumed there had been some mischief, but she was also concerned that possibly her uncle had taken ill in the night. He had looked out of sorts when he went to bed.

She opened the door and was relieved to see it was her uncle stood outside, though the look on his face did not console her for long.

"What is the matter?" She asked him.

"Someone has broken into the house and stolen both skulls," he said, looking bemused as much as he was upset.

Victoria took a second to take in what he had said.

"Someone came in and took two skulls?" she repeated. "Why would anyone steal those?"

"Why indeed?" Bainbridge said, rubbing at his chin, a habit he seemed to have developed while being at the house. "Look, we best go downstairs and take a proper look around the dining room. I thought I had better alert you. I have got Jennings sending men out into the garden to see if they can track anybody. I doubt they will find anyone. They've got a good head start on us, but they might notice where they came in."

"This is preposterous," Victoria said, pulling her dressing gown tighter. "Why would anyone steal skulls? You don't just wander into a house and pick those things up."

"No," said Bainbridge. "Which makes me think they knew they were here, or at least knew one of them was here. The second one only myself and you knew about."

"You are forgetting that Jennings saw us with the second skull," Victoria reminded him. "Are we going to wake up Mr Dunbar?"

Bainbridge had been thinking about that the whole time he had been coming upstairs to wake his niece.

"Probably we should," he said after a moment. "I don't really want to alarm him, but it does seem like something he ought to know about now, rather than in the morning."

"How are you?" Victoria asked, changing the subject, her voice softening as she looked upon her uncle with a frown of concern.

"Me?" Bainbridge said cheerfully. "Why, I'm absolutely fine."

"Then how come you were up in the middle of the night exploring the house and discovering burglars?"

"I couldn't sleep," Bainbridge said honestly.

Victoria gave him a stern look. Bainbridge could always sleep. The fact that he been awake indicated that something had been amiss.

"Do not fret," Bainbridge told her. "I just had an idea, and I had to explore it before I fell asleep. That's all perfectly normal."

"What is not normal is someone slipping into a house and stealing body parts," Victoria gave a shudder. "All right, let's get downstairs and see what's going on. Is Jennings going to alert Mr Dunbar?"

"I shall ask him to. Jennings seems..." Bainbridge paused because he wasn't quite sure what to say next; how had Jennings seemed? "I think it has unsettled him."

"Having intruders in the house would unsettle you," Victoria commented. "It has unsettled me."

"Yes," Bainbridge frowned; there was something else on his mind, but he couldn't quite put his finger on it. "Well, come along then."

They headed back downstairs to the dining room. Now all the gas was lit they could see the room clearly. Bainbridge demonstrated his theory that the intruder had come through one of the windows.

"The latches are very loose, and there is a small gap between the two panes. All it would take is for someone to slip some small object up between them and they could lift the latch and the window would open."

"Quite common in old houses," Victoria nodded. "I have seen such a thing in some of the houses my friends lived in. It was always a concern that it would give easy access for burglars."

"Indeed," Bainbridge toyed with the latch on the window, testing how easily it lifted up. "It is curious they targeted this particular room which contains nothing of value. I don't think they were just any old burglars, you know?"

"You have already mentioned that, and I agree with you," Victoria said. "But how did they know about these skulls?"

"We have limited possibilities on that front," Bainbridge wandered over to the table and touched the spot where the box that held the first skull had once been. "Our first option is that someone happened by the house, looked in the window, saw the skulls, and decided to take them. Though why anyone would decide to steal skulls is quite another matter. Our second option, and the one I feel is more likely, is that someone within this house alerted someone else to these skulls, and for some reason they took them. That limits the likely culprits."

"You are thinking of Jennings," Victoria looked at him sharply. "You think he somehow orchestrated this, perhaps to get Mr Dunbar into trouble?"

"I cannot think why Jennings would organise something like this, but it has crossed my mind," Bainbridge was still rubbing that spot on the table, as if somehow he could feel where the skull had disappeared to, as if answers could be transferred up through his hand. "Apart from us and Mr Dunbar, the only other person who knew about the presence of the skulls was Jennings."

"It is most peculiar," Victoria said, coming over to the table. "Do you suppose Jennings did it to help Mr Dunbar's cousin make a claim upon this house? He could say that the skulls had been shifted out of the house, and that Mr Dunbar was to blame, even though of course he could not have foreseen something like this happening."

"That is a very real possibility. I do hope that is not the case because I fear with the family solicitor firmly on the cousin's side, then this could cause real problems for Mr Dunbar. I hate to think that our endeavours have caused this. I mean, if we had just left the thing up in the attic, then the person would have had a great deal of trouble getting in to steal it."

They were both solemn as Mr Dunbar finally entered the room. He looked flushed in the face. His hair was rumpled and he was clearly not someone who awoke easily in the middle of the night. He tried to flatten his impressive crop of hair.

"What is going on?" he asked. "Jennings was rather mysterious."

Bainbridge waved a hand at the table. Without saying a word he indicated where the skull should have been, and where it now wasn't. Mr Dunbar walked to the table and stared at the empty spot.

"I don't understand," he said. "Where has it gone?"

"There was an intruder," Bainbridge told him, "and they appear to have run off with the skull. But there is more to it than that. This afternoon myself and Victoria headed out to an old family vault, which we learned about in the library..."

"Hang on a moment. A what?"

Bainbridge steadied himself for what was likely to be a lengthy explanation.

"When reading through the archives, we discovered that your family had an old vault installed in the gardens. It was back in the 1600s and within it six people were buried."

Dunbar looked a little faint, and had to settle himself in a chair.

"Just what I need, bodies in the grounds too."

"There is a little more to it than just that," Bainbridge said gently. "When we examined the coffins..."

"You examined the coffins?"

"Mr Dunbar, I have a good explanation for everything we have done, but please let me finish. The most important matter at this moment in time is that when we opened the coffin of Mathias Dunbar, we discovered that he had not been buried on his own. There was a second skull buried with him. This brought us to some very disturbing conclusions. There was a skull in your house, and now an extra skull in a family vault. We had supposed that the skull in the house might have come from that very vault. Instead, it seems that your family had a panache for collecting them.""

You do realise what you are saying?" Dunbar said earnestly. "I mean, this is horrific."

"I appreciate it is not something that anybody wants to hear about their family," Bainbridge admitted. "I am very sorry to have to reveal it to you, but it is simply a matter of fact. In any case, we brought the second skull here, and placed it beside the first. We were going to discuss it with you in the morning. Now both skulls have been stolen."

"This is just utterly preposterous," Dunbar rose and stared at the empty table. "Who would steal a skull, let alone two of them?"

Bainbridge waited to see if Dunbar would realise the answer to his question. It took a moment, then suddenly understanding seemed to dawn on him.

"Oh," said Dunbar. "Oh yes, I see what it could be."

"I am not going to place the blame on Jennings just yet," Bainbridge said quickly. "Not without evidence. The man has always been loyal to your family, and I feel he is loyal to you in his own way."

"Yes, yes, Jennings has been good to me, Bainbridge," Dunbar said firmly. "But even so this... disappearance... it is peculiar and not many people knew about the skull."

"Precisely," Bainbridge nodded. "Tell me, did you let anybody else know apart from us about the discovery?"

Dunbar started to shake his head, then he paused.

"Well, I did write a letter to the family solicitor," he admitted. "When I first discovered the box and its contents, I was rather shaken. I fancied I needed to tell him in case there was some legal matter he would need to attend to. Anyway, I wrote to him a long letter concerning the matter, and he wrote back that it was just another of the family relics I had to keep hold of it as per my aunt's will."

"That raises a host of new possibilities," Bainbridge said glumly. "Of course, I'm not supposing that a solicitor would consider stealing skulls, but he might have mentioned it to your cousin, and he would have reason to do something like this. To imply that you are not capable of protecting the property as your aunt wished."

"No, no, this is just awful," Dunbar had to sit down again. "I cannot believe this is happening. I have barely been here a few weeks, and already terrible things are occurring. A skull in my loft and bodies in my grounds – and now some of them are missing!"

There was not a great deal either of them could do to console him.

"It is unfortunate Mr Dunbar," Bainbridge said gently. "I suggest we all try and get some sleep and return to this in the morning."

"Sleep?" Mr Dunbar said, ironically. "I gave up on that ever since I found that skull!"

Chapter Twelve

The following morning, they came together to hold a council of war. Bainbridge was certain the skull had been stolen in an attempt to discredit Mr Dunbar; he also was convinced that the perpetrator had come from inside the house. He could be wrong, of course, but at that moment in time it seemed the most likely solution. After all, though Mr Dunbar had informed the family solicitor about the skulls, it was highly unlikely that such a man would go sneaking around in the dark. Nor was it likely that Mr Dunbar's cousin had conducted the operation himself. Far more likely that he had paid a servant in the house to do the deed.

The question was, who? Primary on their suspect list was Mr Jennings. So as soon as breakfast had been served, they summoned the old butler into one of the drawing rooms, and there, with Mr Dunbar present, preceded to question him.

"Mr Jennings, you were aware of the skulls residing in the dining room," Bainbridge began.

"I was aware of that unpleasant situation," Mr Jennings admitted.

"It is not my place to say if it was proper or not, but I considered it slightly unhealthy for such objects to be in an area where my late mistress used to enjoy taking her meals."

"This is not about health, Mr Jennings," Bainbridge said. "It is about someone stealing property from this house."

"Yes, Sir. I am deeply concerned about that too, Sir. In all my time here, it is the first occasion when anybody has attempted to sneak into the house. I have always been most conscious about the security of this property, Sir?"

"No, I am afraid, Jennings, that will not do," Bainbridge said sternly. "The problem we have is that the dining room doors were locked. Victoria has explained to me she locked the doors herself yesterday evening and kept the key on her person, the only other key is the spare one that you carry, Mr Jennings."

"Indeed, Sir. I believe we determined that the intruder must have come in through one of the windows?"

"Which is most curious, do you not think?" Bainbridge persisted. "Someone just randomly happened upon this house, saw skulls inside the room, discovered how to open the window, came in and stole them. It is slightly preposterous."

"I would not like to comment on the criminal mind," Jennings said quietly. "It has never been my desire to try and think like a common house breaker."

"Jennings, they think you are behind all this," Mr Dunbar interrupted, finding the interrogation of the old butler too much for him.

He knew where Jennings' true feelings lay, but he also knew that he was loyal to him and to the house. He did not think that the old servant would do something as rascally as perpetrate a robbery on his own property. He was sure it would go against Jennings' feelings for his late mistress, Dunbar's aunt. After all, it was her property he had stolen.

Jennings stared, in what seemed genuine surprise, at his employer.

"That is quite absurd, Sir. In fact, Colonel Bainbridge will be able to verify that I appeared shortly after him to investigate the intrusion."

"That is true," Bainbridge agreed. "However, by the time you appeared, Mr Jennings, the sound from the room had stopped, indicating that the intruder had already departed. I therefore have to consider that you might have slipped out the window, snuck around the back of the house, and then come to find me to pretend that you were not the intruder."

Jennings had a look on his face that implied how remarkable an idea this was, and Victoria had to admit that her uncle's suggestion was quite dramatic. Jennings looked good for his age, but he could not have been far short of eighty, and to suppose that he had been nimbly running around the house and jumping out of windows, then hurrying back to meet up with Bainbridge, did seem slightly absurd.

Dunbar found he could not stand for this talk.

"Colonel, I appreciate what you are saying, but I rather fancy that you are giving too much credit to Mr Jennings. I believe him to be fit and healthy for his age. He is spry for sure, but what you are suggesting seems to me to be slightly beyond even Mr Jennings' remarkable talents."

"What do you have to say for yourself?" Bainbridge turned to the butler, ignoring Dunbar.

"I suppose I should agree with my employer," Jennings said calmly. "I am certainly not as young as I once was, and though I do a good job around the house, I do have my limitations. I have a difficulty with my right knee which would prevent me from clambering in and out of a window."

"We only have your word for that," Bainbridge said, not willing to let the idea go. Sometimes he could be like a dog with a bone.

"True, Sir. I am not quite sure how I could prove it to you, though of course you could ask anybody in the house, namely the housekeeper, who will tell you how often I need to have a hot compress pressed onto my knee to enable me to move around."

"Julius," Victoria turned to her uncle. "Was Mr Jennings out of breath when he reached you?"

Bainbridge hesitated.

"I do not believe that to be the case".

"It would seem to me that anybody who had clambered out of a window and rushed around the house to come to see you, so as to prove they were not the intruder, would certainly be out of breath," Victoria said as gently as she could. "In fact, I would suggest we try it and see just how much effort it would take. If Jennings appeared to you completely calm and without heavy breathing, then surely it indicates that, as he said, he came from the servants quarters rather than dashing around the house?"

Bainbridge had to admit this was a very logical idea. He didn't like the butler. There was something about his demeanour that made Bainbridge feel small, and perhaps that was clouding his judgement. He recalled how much effort it had cost him the day before just going to the vault and back, and how Jennings was older than him by more than a decade. The more he considered it, the more he appreciated what Victoria was saying, and that Jennings did not seem likely to have been the intruder.

"Very well. Your argument is sound," he said reluctantly to his niece. "However, Jennings, I think we have to assume that someone within this house took those skulls."

"Sir?" Jennings said, glancing towards his employer.

"On that front, I do believe he is correct," Dunbar said. "There are very few people who know about the presence of the skulls in this house. I fear that one of the servants may have been coerced into removing them. Presumably by my cousin, or at least by the family solicitor. I am very disappointed about all this."

Mr Dunbar slumped in his chair, looking as disappointed as he sounded. There was a slight change in Jennings' expression.

"I am very sorry about all this, Sir. I always felt that the servants were most loyal to you. I shall, of course, question them."

"The simplest solution would be to dismiss everyone," Bainbridge remarked, catching the butler's attention. He had intended to do exactly that. "If you cannot trust one of them, you cannot trust all of them. That's the way of things."

"Oh, surely not," Dunbar said, looking worried. "Some of them have been with the family decades. I don't suppose they could find a position elsewhere."

"It is a question of trust," Bainbridge told him. "They have placed you in a terrible position. What might they do next?"

Jennings was listening keenly, worried about all this talk of dismissing the servants. He felt protective to his fellow employees. He was desperate to say something, but as a good butler, he knew it was against protocol for him to speak, unless directly spoken to.

He tried to catch Victoria's eye, hoping that she might understand what he wanted, and so address him. He succeeded, raising an eyebrow at her when she looked his way. Victoria, who was very familiar with the ways of servants, understood.

"Perhaps we shall ask Mr Jennings' thoughts on all this?" she said distracting her uncle. "Mr Jennings?"

"Well, my lady," Jennings said, relieved that she had realised what he wanted. "It would seem to me that if someone in this household is working against Mr Dunbar, it is imperative for all of us to locate them at once. It causes a great stain on my conscience, and upon my honour, to think that someone is doing this. I would like to be given the opportunity to help in finding out who perpetrated this crime."

"The problem we have, Mr Jennings," Bainbridge told him coldly, "is that you are under suspicion as much as the other servants, while you may not have entered that room and stolen the skulls yourself, you surely could have orchestrated it. You have the power to command someone else in this house to do exactly as you wish."

Jennings nodded his head.

"I appreciate that, Sir, and of course there is not much I can do other than to give my word that it was not me. However, I still ask that you allow me to assist in trying to find out who committed this crime. And to do this before such a drastic action is taken as dismissing all the servants. It would be a shame, as so many have been loyal all these years, for them all to be stained by someone's foolish actions."

"He is correct," Dunbar said keenly. "I don't want to blame all the servants when it is surely just one who is responsible."

"Then I suppose we are agreed," Bainbridge concluded. "However, there is quite a bit we must do and, Jennings, you must be more forthcoming. Until this point, you have been reluctant to speak freely to us, now that must change. You need to be open and clear about anything you know concerning these strange relics."

"Yes, Sir. I understand, Sir," Jennings promised him. "For the sake of us all, I shall make sure that I am always honest with you. It is not in my nature and my position to speak freely, as you put it, but if that is what you require, and you give me permission, I will help you."

Victoria gave him a gentle smile. She felt he did indeed mean that.

"We need to begin by understanding how exactly the intruder got into the room and took the skulls," Bainbridge said. "Victoria locked the doors of the dining room yesterday and took the key with her. The only other person to have a key is you, Mr Jennings, I believe."

"You are correct, Sir," Jennings informed him. "I keep a master key for all the rooms, just in case."

"And there are no extra keys that might have been made at some point? Many old houses have quite a collection of keys hanging around."

"No, Sir. We always try to keep good track of all the keys just to be on the safe side. I can show you my key ring if you would like."

"No need for that, Jennings," Dunbar told him. "We know you have it. I trust you."

He was trying to demonstrate that he was willing to side with his servant and put his faith behind him. Jennings looked relieved that in this regard he was at least being trusted.

"I know you had your key with you when you arrived at the doors," Bainbridge said. "Seeing as you unlocked the doors for us. Which leaves us with a conundrum. Either a servant did as we supposed and clambered in through the window or they had access to a spare key."

"The keys are never out of my safe keeping," Jennings insisted.

"Well, that leaves one key. Victoria, where is the key you took from the dining room doors?"

Victoria quickly went into the pocket of her dress and felt around for the key. It was then she realised it was gone.

"It is missing!" She said, appalled she had not noticed before. "Someone must have taken it."

There was a strange look on Dunbar's face, as if he didn't quite believe her. Victoria felt awful. She had locked the doors and meant to keep the key to ensure that nothing could happen to the skulls, and now it appeared that she had been the weak link in the household security.

"I am so very sorry," she told them.

Chapter Thirteen

Victoria was despondent that she had failed to keep hold of the key. The thought that someone must have searched her dress pocket at some point during the night worried her deeply. She had worn her dress to dinner, and had then retired while still wearing it. She had undressed, and left the gown lying on a chair. If someone had slipped in and stolen the key, it meant they had been in her room while she was sleeping. The only other option was to surmise they had somehow picked her pocket while she was about the house, and she did not think that was possible.

Bainbridge endeavoured to console her.

"It is a good thing, in all honesty. It means that we know for certain that it must be someone within this house who is behind the crime. After all, they had to be in this house to steal that key."

"Might I also interposed that they must have known the young lady had the key upon her," Jennings added. "Which was not something I was aware of."

"I had not mentioned that I had taken the key to anyone," Victoria insisted. "However, I suppose someone might have seen me take the key. I wasn't exactly discreet about it. My mind was preoccupied thinking that I would prefer it if the skulls were behind locked doors."

Oh yes," Mr Dunbar said in a strange tone. "I have similar feelings like that. It is very consoling to know that they are behind a lock, and that they cannot get out on their own."

They all looked in his direction. Even Jennings gave his master a slightly curious glance.

"What? You have never considered that there might be something supernatural about them?" Dunbar asked them. "After all, who goes around putting skulls in their house? No, no, I feel quite certain it is better that they are behind locked doors. In fact, I am mildly relieved they aren't in this house at all."

"Not in this house," Bainbridge said, raising a finger. Victoria glanced at her uncle, waiting for the next part of that sentence.

"Why yes, that would make good sense," he continued thoughtfully, as if they weren't there at all.

"Might you care to elaborate on what is going through your mind?" Victoria asked him.

Bainbridge had a strange smile on his face.

"Look at it this way," he said. "Someone took those skulls, but where did they put them? I mean the grounds of the estate are vast. A person could hide them somewhere there, but it is a lot of work. The culprit would have to dig a hole and, as far as we are aware, none of the servants know about the family vault. No, no, the more I consider it, the more it would make sense to simply remove the skulls from the dining room and place them somewhere else within the house. The result is the same. Mr Dunbar is upset and it can be claimed the items have left the property. Depending on what is planned for the skulls after their removal, it might be rather convenient to hide them somewhere within the property."

"You mean the skulls could still be here?" Mr Dunbar said, suddenly brightening.

"I think that is a distinct possibility," Bainbridge nodded. "At the very least, it would be careless of us not to hunt through the house, just to be on the safe side."

"Sir, that is a very wise idea," Jennings agreed. "It would give me an opportunity to speak to the servants discreetly, without them being aware of your concerns. We could say that we think the items have been misplaced at some point. We might say that perhaps someone thought they would clean the box. It would be quite proper for me to make enquiries about the matter, and we can search the house from top to bottom."

"I would certainly be relieved if they were found so easily," Mr Dunbar said. "Though I can't say I would be relieved that they were still in this house."

For a brief moment, he had been quite happy in the notion that the skulls were no longer inside his property, even though the consequences of their disappearance could be quite serious. Sometimes the desire to have a good night's sleep can override anything else, including common sense.

"We might also have a look for the second key to the dining room," Bainbridge added. "After all, it must have been put somewhere. If it is not simply stashed in a drawer where no one has thought to look, then it may be still on the person who took it."

"If you do not mind," Victoria interrupted. "I should like to be in charge of searching for the key. I feel it is my responsibility."

"You must not take it to heart that you were the victim of a robbery," Bainbridge told her gently. "It could have happened to any of us. After all, you did not think that someone in this household would do such a thing."

"Yet, I should have done," Victoria was not going to forgive herself so easily. "I should have realised that it could be someone within the servants who was working against Mr Dunbar. After all, we had thought that Jennings…"

She tailed off quickly, but her words were already out there. The old butler simply nodded at her.

"Yes, my lady, I understand. You considered that I might be working against Mr Dunbar."

"I do not consider that now," Victoria told him firmly. "It was just something that crossed our minds initially. After all, you seemed the likeliest person… No, that sounds wrong. I am so sorry, Jennings. That is not what I mean to say."

"I do not take offence," Jennings said gently. "I have been told far worse during the course of my time as a servant."

"May I ask, Jennings," Bainbridge began, "why you felt it so remiss that Mr Dunbar here should inherit the house over his cousin?"

"It is not my place to speak about such matters," Jennings suddenly became closed lipped, despite the fact he had been speaking quite freely for several minutes.

"Now, now, Jennings, we agreed that you would speak openly and I have asked you a direct question," Bainbridge pointed out.

Jennings glanced at his master, pursing his lips; it was clear he did not want to speak his thoughts.

"Go ahead Jennings, I shall not take offence," Mr Dunbar told him cheerfully. "I'm quite used to people saying things against me. Really, you have to be quite cheerful about it. All through my life I've been considered the lowliest relative in the family."

Mr Dunbar did not seem to be bothered by his own comment. Jennings was at last persuaded to speak.

"It is a simple matter of tradition," he told Bainbridge. "My mistress inherited this house from her father. That was logical because she was a spinster and would have had nowhere else to go. But it should have gone to the eldest direct male relative after that. Over the course of the years, I have known Mr Dunbar's cousin very well. He has visited the house regularly since childhood. I suppose I grew quite accustomed to the idea that one day he would be living here. Then along came Mr Dunbar, who was something of an oddity in all this. He is different from the family. I cannot quite explain what different means in that sense, but it is what it is. He came along and it was like having someone new intruding on things, rather like that intruder coming into the dining room, it felt like he was interposing himself."

"You thought I was a money grabber," Mr Dunbar noted. "Well, that is quite understandable. I can see how you would think that."

Mr Dunbar's great cheer at saying this rather threw Jennings, it also raised him up in the old butler's regard.

"I do believe, Sir, I have been rather unkind towards you. Unchristian, in fact. I was not prepared to give you a chance. I made a snap judgement about you rather than allowing you the opportunity to prove yourself."

"In that regard, I think it's safe to say we have done something similar," Victoria said to Jennings. "We made a snap judgement about you, Mr Jennings. I think we can all see that sometimes our first impressions are not what they should be."

"Very wise words, my lady," Jennings nodded. "My point is that I am beginning to warm to Mr Dunbar, and I can see why my late mistress considered him the proper owner for this house. He does seem to be very interested in keeping the house in the family and making sure it is well maintained."

"Thank you, Jennings. You do not know how much that means

to me," Mr Dunbar grinned at the butler. "All through my life, most people have considered me pretty worthless. Not much good for anything. I was just the one that tottered along in the background. I was the cheerful one, the jolly one, but perhaps the one not seen as being terribly sensible. I only made connection with my aunt because I wanted to know more about my father. It is nice to think that I am, perhaps, finally finding my place in this world."

"Now you're being too harsh on yourself," Bainbridge said to Dunbar. "You are clearly a decent fellow, but we need to go back to this matter of the skulls. Someone in this house has taken them and we need to discover who it is. We are all agreed we are working together?"

He glanced around the room, and everybody nodded their heads.

"Then we must begin at once. We should divide the house into sections. Mr Jennings, I believe it is advisable that you search the servants' quarters."

"Yes, Sir," Jennings nodded, agreeing.

"I believe I should go with him and look through the servants' personal belongings," Victoria said. "After all, it would be improper for a man to search the female servants' belongings, and I need to find out where that key is."

"I am sure I can figure out some excuse for the lady to be down there," Jennings said.

"Very well, that leaves me and Mr Dunbar. I shall search search the ground floor and, Mr Dunbar, you can search the first floor with the bedrooms. I doubt we're going to find anything up in the main quarters, but you never know. We should leave the attic to last, and there we shall all convene to have another discussion about what we have learned."

They all agreed this was a proper plan. Mr Dunbar was quite cheerful about the whole matter, seeing it as something of an adventure. Victoria just wanted to redeem herself, feeling she had failed by losing the key. They all agreed to meet again later in the day, and set about their various tasks.

Chapter Fourteen

J ennings led Victoria down into the servants' quarters.

"They shall not be expecting you, my lady. They will perhaps think it odd, but I shall come up with some excuse," he told her as they headed down.

Like most old houses, the servants' quarters were partly below ground and at the back of the house. They interconnected with the old cellars and rooms that consisted of kitchens, pantries, an old dairy that was not in great use, and various rooms for the laundry. It was also where the servants slept.

The house retained a small staff. Mr Dunbar's late aunt had not required many people to look after her, however, she had kept on a number of old retainers out of kindness, and because she knew they would have nowhere else to go. When a servant reaches a certain age, then it becomes difficult to place them elsewhere, and they are unlikely to have a home to go to. Therefore, if the family is not kind enough to allow them to stay on and undertake minor tasks to give them purpose, they could end up homeless.

Mr Dunbar's aunt had thought greatly of the servants that had served her and her father in his dotage. Some of them she had known since she was a girl herself. Though, those were diminishing in number as they aged. They either grew so unwell they had to go to the workhouse or the cottage hospital, or they simply died. Jennings was now the oldest remaining servant in the house.

The next oldest was the housekeeper, Mrs Moss, who had been with the family for the last fifty years. She knew all the ways of the household, all the things they liked to eat, the daily routine, even down to the way the stove needed to be lit in a very particular fashion so that it took first time. She had trained up most of the other servants in the kitchen; all of them apart from the old valet, Mr Jones, who had always been under Jennings' tuition.

Jones was the next oldest. He was a spry man in his late fifties who still acted something like a boy. He had never progressed beyond valet, though he could have at one time become a butler. Instead, he had been happy to retain his current post, especially as once the old master had died, he had very little to actually do. He mainly lurked around the kitchen, getting under Mrs Moss' feet, and doing any task that Jennings found too tiresome, such as making sure the old hinges of the outhouse were well oiled, or moving the compost heap. In this way he had a purpose but was not overly taxed.

Then there were three household maids, the youngest and newest members of the household. None were above the age of twenty-five. They were under the supervision of Mrs Moss and performed the usual household duties; making sure the beds were made, cleaning the fireplaces, sweeping, dusting, tidying. They did not have a great deal to do as many of the rooms were unused, though it was hoped that once Mr Dunbar fully moved in with his new wife, and they had a family, the household should be quite busy once again.

The only other person in the house was a strange little fellow simply known as Imp. At first glance, Imp might have been assumed to be a child; in fact, he was an adult of incredibly small stature and this was blamed upon an acute childhood illness and lack of nutrition. He also retained a very boyish appearance, though he was now well into his thirties. Imp had never told the family his actual name. He had arrived one day looking for work, and Mr Dunbar's aunt had felt so sorry for the poor fellow, who was at that time shoeless and walking around in ragged clothes, that she hired him on the spot. Quite what she had hired him to do was always questionable.

Imp was useful in his own way; he was nimble with his fingers and was always ready to perform any task. He attended to any job with great speed and enthusiasm, though not always with the greatest success. It was not that he was clumsy, it was just that he seemed to make a lot of mistakes whenever doing anything. No one quite knew what to make of him. His name for one was so curious, yet it was the only one he ever went by. It was assumed that at some point he might have been with a travelling show, the sort where poor folk with unusual afflictions were forced to sit before the public and present themselves as exhibitions. Whatever the case, he was a resident of the household and the others would be loyal to him to the end of their days.

These were the people that constituted the inside staff. The outside staff included the gardeners, but at this point Victoria was dismissing them from her enquiries, as they would not have had ready access to the main house. Gardeners would come into the kitchen for their meals, and possibly use some of the spare storage rooms for their tools and other belongings, but they would not be allowed to go around the house, and any doing so would be accosted. It seemed unlikely one of them had managed to sneak into the dining room. That left the six members of the main staff to consider as suspects.

Mr Jennings appeared in the kitchen and Mrs Moss was about to say something to him when she spied Victoria just behind him. Her expression became closed, and she turned back to focusing on the sauce she was preparing ready for the pie she was baking later in the day. She had discovered that Bainbridge was quite keen on pies, and all good housekeepers are fond of having someone to cook for, it is in their nature, so she was gladly honing her pie making skills again.

"I believe you are all aware of our guests in the house," Mr Jennings addressed the members of the household staff.

All the servants, bar one of the maids, were currently in the kitchen. It was just after the family breakfast, when the staff would have their own breakfast and a cup of tea before getting on with their tasks for the day. The maids had already been up since dawn cleaning and blacking the grates. The one maid who was missing was currently visiting the outhouse.

"I have made the special request of asking Miss Bovington to come down into the kitchen because I have heard of a strange incident that I must address immediately," Jennings continued. "It has come to my attention that someone was in the house last night, someone who should not have been here, and something was taken. Only a small something, but it was stolen nonetheless. This object, we believe, may still be in the house because the intruder was disturbed and could not have simply slipped away. We fear he may have stumbled down to the servants' quarters and hidden the object among our possessions, to try and cast blame upon us for the crime.

"The sad truth is that Mr Dunbar is currently under attack from another member of his family who wishes to discredit him. He currently only has us to aid him and be his allies, so it appears to be the motive of this unfortunate relative to try and force Mr Dunbar to turn against us, those he can most trust. If he were to get rid of us, after all, who would he have left to take care of him? He would have to hire new people; new people that could be easily influenced by the disagreeable relative.

"Mr Dunbar is a very kind gentleman, and he has agreed with me that he does not want to cast suspicion where it should not fall. He has consented to my suggestion that all our belongings be searched in a proper fashion so that it can be clearly and plainly proved to anyone who may question us, that we were not responsible for this act. He is in full confidence of your loyalty, as am I. This is purely a matter to try and prevent those who would discredit him, and us, from raising suspicions. It is very important we do this to avoid these enemies causing unnecessary disruption."

The servants listened in silence, deeply moved by what he was saying, which caused Victoria a pang of unease; they all looked, for want of a better word, innocent.

"I have imposed on Miss Bovington to be the person to conduct the search. Since it would be improper for me to search among the ladies' belongings, and also it provides an unbiased witness. I hope therefore you will give her your kind cooperation and that this can be over and done with in a speedy fashion."

"So you are saying, Mr Jennings," spoke up old Mr Jones, "that this here fellow intruded into the house and stole something just so he could plant it on one of us and make us look bad?"

"It is just one theory," Jennings explained, "because the item that was taken was far too curious and of little value to warrant a regular burglar stealing it. It may be that the object was removed from the house entirely, but we want to be sure they aren't trying to cast blame where it should not fall."

"Well, that is understandable," Mrs Moss said firmly. "The servants always get the blame for being thieves. It is the way of things, and I have heard that Mr Dunbar's cousin is quite reprehensible in that fashion. He goes through servants like nobody's business. I would not care to work for him. I was very relieved when our mistress decided that Mr Dunbar should inherit this house."

"Now, now, Mrs Moss, you should not speak so of someone else," Mr Jennings said gently, even though he had been encouraging them to be dismissive of Mr Dunbar's cousin.

"I say things as I see them, I always have," Mrs Moss remarked. "Now we need to get to the end of this mischief once and for all. You can begin by taking a look around my room if you wish to Miss Bovington. I have nothing to hide, and if you do discover this item in there, well, I should like to know how any intruder dared to come into my bedroom."

Imp had a wicked smile on his face and nearly chuckled out loud at this statement. Mr Jones gave him a sharp nudge with his elbow.

"Very well, Mrs Moss, we shall begin with you, and move through the household. With any luck, the item will come to light upstairs at some point, where my master and Colonel Bainbridge are searching."

"It is terrible to think someone was lurking about last night," Mrs Moss persisted. "I heard you getting up, Mr Jennings, so I knew something was afoot."

"Well, let us hope we can resolve this in a speedy fashion and that no more bother shall occur," Jennings said placidly. "Now, Mrs Moss, would you kindly show Miss Bovington to your room?"

Chapter Fifteen

Bainbridge wandered around the ground floor of the house, looking for possible entry points that an intruder might have used. Of course, he was pretty confident that, as the perpetrator had come from inside the house, it would not be necessary to have gained entry illicitly, but it was always prudent to look for these things. He was starting to wonder just how many intrusions might have occurred in the house without anybody being aware. Though Jennings had said this was the first time an intruder had been in the property, it was entirely possible that he had been mistaken. Jennings, after all, was an old man whose hearing was perhaps not once what it was, and a cunning intruder may just as easily have snuck in through a different part of the house and not woken the butler. Who else, after all, would have noticed them? Mr Dunbar slept upstairs and, until recently, had been a sound sleeper. The other servants were below stairs and unlikely to hear a thing. No, Bainbridge had to postulate that there was a possibility Jennings may have failed to have heard other intrusions.

Bainbridge was working on the theory that Mr Dunbar's cousin might have tried to disrupt his claim on the house before. There was all this business about things not being removed from the house; how easy it would be to cause Mr Dunbar trouble if some suitable item was removed. There was that whole business about the attic never being cleared. Now, if an intruder were to get up there and take something significant, say, a family photo album, something that might be worth a little bit of money, but could also be proven to have come from the house, and then if it showed up at, say, a pawn shop or some other such place, it could be said that Mr Dunbar had gone completely against his aunt's wishes. The family solicitor, Mr Haggerton, would make it very difficult for Mr Dunbar to defend himself.

However, getting up into the attic was harder than it might seem, because that would require the intruder slipping past Mr Dunbar's bedroom. He would be walking around in a space above where the gentleman slept and Bainbridge was familiar enough with attics to know they usual had very creaky boards and footsteps echoed very easily within them.

After all, you could often hear rats in attics, and if you could hear rats, you would surely hear a person stomping about.

Bainbridge walked about the house, checking windows, and noting how easy any one of them would be to enter from the outside. None of them had locks, and most were of the old fashioned latch type; the latch being quite loose and flimsy. In fact, he found with a few, that with a suitable nudge you could get the latch to jump up and the window to open. There was nothing to prevent anybody from getting inside if they truly wished. That the house had not been burgled before was actually quite remarkable, after all, it contained enough valuable items to attract a thief.

There was silverware in some of the drawers, and items of value on nearly every shelf. It would not take long for an intruder to slip in, collect a few small items in their pockets, and slip away again to sell them. Bainbridge supposed it was the simple fact that no one really knew about this house, or its contents, that had protected it all these years. Having done a thorough patrol of the ground floor, he returned to the dining room and once again found himself looking at that window they thought the intruder had slipped out.

He played through scenarios in his head. The servant had somehow stolen the key from Victoria. It was either done during dinner, when the servants were passing around plates and perhaps one had proven themselves a good pickpocket, or it had been done after Victoria was soundly asleep. The intruder would have come down the stairs and unlocked the door to the dining room, probably using the entry in the back corridor, rather than the one that led off the main hall. It would be more discreet and less likely they would be noticed. They locked the door behind them just to be on the safe side, and also to throw off the scent. Then all they had to do was pick up the skulls, carry them to the window, open the window, clamber out, go round the house...

Bainbridge paused; an idea had just come to him, and it was a curious one. He was considering how awkwardly shaped the skull box was. How cumbersome it had been to carry when they had brought it down from the attic. Mr Dunbar had manhandled it down to the ground floor with some effort. The box had been made from sturdy, solid wood, and it was an unusual size to fit the skull suitably. It was heavy too.

To suppose that an intruder had skilfully got out of a window without making some sort of noise was an interesting idea. Especially as there were two skulls they had to remove. Bainbridge went to the window and opened it again, looking outside. There was a gravel path all around the outside of the house. Bainbridge cursed himself as he noted this. Well, of course, he should have been aware of it before.

Gravel paths were one of the big deterrents for a would be burglar because, even with the greatest of skill, it was impossible not to make some sort of sound on a gravel path. Footsteps on gravel, were easy to hear. The sort of thing people picked up on a quiet, still night. It was a very simple, and cheap, means of deterring intruders.

But of course, if there were gravel outside, why had he not heard someone on it? He thought about things for a moment. He was certain that no one had hung around in the dining room. There were simply no hiding places they could conceal themselves in. He started to look a bit more closely around the room in the daylight. There was an old sideboard, but it did not have a solid body. Instead, pillars allowed an open area beneath the drawers. The only other potential hiding places were a small cupboard where crockery was kept. When Bainbridge opened this, he found that there were shelves inside. Again, it would have been impossible for someone to squeeze themselves in. No, the more he looked, the more it seemed likely the intruder had slipped out the window. But then, if that were the case, why had he not heard them on the gravel? Had he been so distracted by Jennings' arrival that he simply overlooked it?

He let himself out of the house and headed around to the window. Then he stopped and looked at the gravel patch beneath the window. Gravel does not retain footprints and so it was impossible to see if someone had stood there. What he did note was a mark on the grass verge just beyond the path.

If he was not mistaken, someone had dropped a heavy item hastily down on the grass in an effort to avoid it landing on the gravel and making a sound. It had left two slight indentations where the corners had clipped into the soil. Bainbridge slowly realised what might have occurred. Supposing the intruder had tossed the box out of the window so it landed on the grass? Then they had managed to stand on the window frame and jump across onto the grass as well.

It could be done, he thought to himself. The issue was that the window had been closed when they entered the room, implying the intruder had been able to shut it after they left. How could they have done that *and* avoided stepping on the gravel? He started to look around, nearby there was a hydrangea bush, and it was thick with blooms. When he examined it closely, to his surprise, his hand fell on something long and hard; he drew out what was an old walking stick. Well, yes, he thought to himself. That would do the trick.

He could reach it across the gravel path and push the window shut, knowing how loose the latch was, with a little bit of jiggling, the window would have secured itself. Then all the intruder had to do was slip away on the grass quietly. All this, of course, implied someone who was very nimble and light on their feet. They also were unlikely to have been encumbered by skirts. Bainbridge thought that women could do some pretty impressive manoeuvres while wearing skirts, but he was also well aware that they were an obstacle to true athleticism.

Performing the feat he had just envisioned, standing on the window sill and leaping across to the grass beyond, was something that could not be performed in a restrictive skirt. It meant either the intruder was male, and that certainly narrowed down the suspects, or it was a woman who had opted to wear trousers. That, in itself, was quite a remarkable thing, though it was not the first time he had heard of such a case.

He looked around for a while longer, trying to find any trace of where the box, or the intruder, had stood. He thought he could make out very slight marks in the soft ground heading away from the window. But it could also have been a trick of the light. There was nothing else in the hydrangea bush.

Satisfied that he had discovered all there was to discover concerning the window and the intruder's departure, Bainbridge headed back inside and continued his prowl around the ground floor. He was no longer looking for signs of intrusion, but to get some feel and sense for which one of the servants might be inclined to help Mr Dunbar's cousin. There had to be a reason why he had been betrayed. It could have been financial, of course, but a truly loyal servant would not be swayed by money, not when they knew their position was so safe and secure at the house. Mr Dunbar was quite clearly keen to keep his servants on, after all. Servants did not give up such positions lightly, especially servants who had been with the household a long time.

No, to betray Mr Dunbar, as had happened, he suspected there was something deeper going on, perhaps some deep grudge. Someone settling old business; perhaps, whatever had occurred had happened during Dunbar's aunt's time, and it was nothing Dunbar had done that had caused the servant to favour his cousin. It was difficult, however, to determine anything just looking at the house; all he saw was a very pristinely arranged place. A home that was both comfortable and practical.

He eventually came to a writing table in one of the rooms and opened the lid to look inside. It had belonged to Mr Dunbar's aunt, and she had kept all her correspondence from the last couple of years within it. He was soon plodding through drafts of the letters she had written to Mr Dunbar, and the ones that had been written back, in the hopes that he might discover some clue as to why a servant would wish to betray him.

He was still there when Mr Dunbar wandered into the room.

"I am having difficulty in my search, Bainbridge," Dunbar admitted. "I started determinedly enough, but I now find myself searching with ever increasing dread that I might actually find something. I do not believe I can go on looking for these skulls within the house alone. I am too afraid of finding them."

Bainbridge realised he should have considered Dunbar's aversion for the skulls when sending him off to look for them alone. That he had found the task too disagreeable was somewhat unsurprising.

"Perhaps, then we should combine forces," he conceded gently. "I confess, I have my own difficulties when searching as I do not bend as well as I used to."

"We should help each other," Dunbar nodded. "Together we shall be considerably more efficient."

"Quite," Bainbridge said. "Let us head back upstairs then."

With that, he gave up on the correspondence and followed Mr Dunbar back through the rooms, silently complaining to himself that yet again he was going to have to face climbing stairs unnecessarily.

Chapter Sixteen

Mrs Moss escorted Victoria to her bedroom.

"I do find it most disturbing that something in the house has gone missing," she said, bustling her through and pointing out where she kept her belongings.

The room contained a wardrobe, a small bed with a metal bedstead, and a small chest of drawers beside it. There was not much else aside from a very old chair that sat in the corner with a book perched on the arm. The book, when Victoria took a closer look, was a work of poetry.

"All the years I have worked here, no one has ever broken into the house," Mrs Moss continued. She sat herself down on her old bed, which creaked beneath her. "I have been here since I was a girl, you know. Back then, it seemed a different place. That was when old Mr Dunbar was alive. His wife was still around then too, and the older boys, though they were not here long before they moved out and went their own ways. I remember the current Mr Dunbar's father very well. A sweet lad, perhaps a little bit naïve, but on the whole I liked him a good deal. I should say I liked him better than his older brother. Though there was nothing particularly wrong with him, just that he was aloof and did not seem to care much what the servants got up to, or how they felt about life.

"I know it is rather peculiar to say such things, but a servant does notice when they are cared about. And though many a householder would assume that a servant was just a tool, something no different really to a sophisticated fire poker, to a servant it means a lot when the family cares about them. It alters the way we work for a start, at least, I think so. I would not have been here all this time had I felt uncared for, and certainly Mr Jennings would not have stayed. The old master was very, very good to us, and so was his daughter."

Mrs Moss became solemn. She stared at the walls of her room, which were papered in a pattern of small rosebuds and green stripes. She seemed to be looking beyond them. To another time, another place. Remembering who had gone before them, and who was now lost to her.

"Mr Dunbar seems very nice," Victoria said to try to nudge her out of her morbidity.

Mrs Moss glanced at her.

"Oh yes, he is very nice, and I am sure he will have a lovely wife, and they will have a family here, and it will be quite something. The house will bustle again, and that will be very nice. Very nice."

There was something in the way she spoke that made Victoria feel she did not entirely mean that, perhaps after all these years of growing used to serving a single elderly woman, Mrs Moss was not feeling comfortable with the idea of having a young family in the house again. Perhaps she was wondering about the amount of work it would require from her, and whether she could keep up. She was not a young woman herself. She was in her dotage, and so were her fellow servants, apart from the maids. Maybe it was time to consider retirement, but where would she go? Victoria imagined that was the peril of many a long standing servant.

"Do you know much about the things that were kept up in the attic?" She asked, again trying to draw the housekeeper away from her sad thoughts.

"When I was younger I used to be sent up there to dust," Mrs Moss commented. "Which was a strange thing, because I thought to myself who else would go up there? But it was always very dusty, so I suppose it had a point. I used to feel it was a punishment, or a task to keep me out of the way when something else was happening."

"There is certainly a lot of stuff up there," Victoria added trying to draw something from the woman.

"The family have lived here a long time," Mrs Moss said. "You collect things over such a length of time, especially when you have the money for it. The old Mr Dunbar was a collector of many things. He showed me the shells he had bought from all across the world. And then he had his rock collection, and there were also a vast number of books. I suppose it must run in the family to collect things, and once you have collected them, you cannot really get rid of them. So that's why everything ended up in the attic."

"Talking about collecting things, did Mr Dunbar senior have any interest in human anatomy and the collecting of objects relating to people?"

Victoria was not sure it was quite the right question, but she was trying to be as gentle as possible when it came to asking about whether Mrs Moss had heard that her former employer collected skulls.

"I don't think I quite know what you mean," Mrs Moss said. "He liked inanimate objects – shells, stones. He had quite a range of pressed leaves in a book. He liked look at them to try to discover how the various trees related to one another. Did a Sycamore bear similarities to a Birch tree and stuff like that. He collected natural objects as well. Things like rabbit pelts, and stuffed birds, though he got rid of them towards the end of his days, he said they made him feel rather ancient himself. He didn't like looking at dead things anymore. They were one of the few things he actually did get rid of, when I come to think about it."

For a man who did not like dead things, Victoria mused, Mr Dunbar had seemed quite happy to retain an old skull up in his attic, not to mention the family crypt, though possibly he was unware of that.

"Where would you care to look first," Mrs Moss asked

Victoria was fairly confident she was not going to find a skull in Mrs Moss' room, but for the sake of form and to encourage the other servants to follow suit with the search she knew she had to take a look around.

"Well, I think I should start with the wardrobe," she said, opening the doors and looking inside.

She was not surprised that it contained an assortment of dresses and pressed aprons ready for the housekeeper's work. There was a box at the bottom which, when she opened it, contained a fancy hat; one for wearing to church on Sundays and out on special trips. There was an umbrella, a second pair of shoes and a pair of gloves. There was also a coat for the winter, but apart from that there was very little else.

"You are perhaps thinking that it seems very few belongings for someone who has spent a lifetime here," Mrs Moss said, and there was again that hint of wistful sadness in her voice.

Victoria closed the doors of the wardrobe and turned back to the housekeeper.

"Not everyone is a collector of mementoes," she said, trying to be soothing.

"Not everyone has the chance to collect mementoes," Mrs Moss replied. "I have been in this house a long time, and certainly I have collected memories. When it comes to objects, very few have come through my hands. I have never really bought much for myself. Never really acquired gifts from people. Perhaps if I had been more of an outgoing person, I should have some correspondence of interest to show you, but even that is lacking. The odd Christmas card, maybe, but apart from that, nothing much else. I always tended to think of this house as a whole as belonging to me. Not that I meant it belonged to me, you understand, because that would be improper. But rather I looked upon the possessions within it as somehow in my keeping, something I looked after and that made-up for a lack of personal items, if you see what I mean?"

Victoria did see what she meant, though she still could not help feeling the housekeeper's sadness.

"I shall look in the chest of drawers now," she said, feeling awkward.

Mrs Moss shuffled along the bed to give her room and Victoria went to the cabinet and gently looked through the drawers. She felt uneasy looking at someone else's personal items. There were underclothes in one drawer, stockings in another. She also spotted a silver backed hairbrush and a small mirror. There was a container of hairgrips, and another fancy box that contained hatpins. She noted to herself there were no signs of photographs, or anything that indicated that Mrs Moss had a life outside of the house. No signs of a family, no letters to friends. Nothing. It seemed that the Dunbars had been her whole world, and for a long time that had suited her.

"I should just peer under the bed," Victoria added and dropped to her knees to look.

Not to her surprise, there wasn't much other than an old, battered suitcase which she quietly pulled out. It felt light and she assumed it was empty.

"Just in case I do have to travel anywhere," Mrs Moss explained to her. "There is a key somewhere for it, of course."

Mrs Moss tapped her lower lip and looked around the room. Then she jumped off the bed and headed to a coat hanging on a hook in the corner. She fumbled in a pocket and produced a key, which she handed to Victoria. Victoria tried it in the locks on the suitcase and they popped open. She looked inside and found it was empty, as she had expected.

"Not much is there? Not much to say I had a life."

Victoria glanced up at Mrs Moss.

"I think we all have our regrets like that," she said. "For many of us, we wonder, what mark did we make on this world? What did we do to be remembered? I don't think you should begrudge that. I think it's just, well, natural. Especially when you have lost someone recently you were very close to."

There was the faintest hint of tears in Mrs Moss' eyes, but of course, she was far too professional to ever cry in front of someone who could be classified as an employer or at least a guest of her employer.

"When I began here, I was only a little younger than the late Mrs Dunbar," She explained. "I tended to always think of her like a sister. Over the years we became very close, talked about a lot of things. It is hard to think she is gone. I didn't feel lonely until she departed this world. But then I suppose that is what it is like to be with an actual sister all these years."

Mrs Moss's sadness was infectious and Victoria was starting to think of her own family and her uncle and the worries she had recently had about his health.

"You will figure out who is doing all this to poor Mr Dunbar, won't you?" Mrs Moss said. "It is a terrible thing and it upsets us deeply. I just wish everything could return to normal."

"Well, we are here to work this out, and I have no doubt we will," Victoria said, as confidently as she could manage. "We always do solve a mystery. My uncle is very good at it."

Mrs Moss nodded.

"I think it is time we were getting on," she added. "Who's room would you like to search next?"

Chapter Seventeen

"I really cannot fathom any of this," Mr Dunbar said as they walked upstairs. "It is not so much the keeping of the skull if it was Oliver Cromwell's, but the fact that there are now two of them."

"These mysteries do occur in families with a long lineage," Bainbridge assured him. "In my own family, for instance, there is a mysterious old box which is said to have once contained the ashes of a certain famous admiral. How it came into the possession of the Bainbridges is quite beyond me."

"I see your point, but there's a difference between ashes and a skull," Dunbar said, then he considered for a moment and decided that perhaps it wasn't so different. "What is this obsession people have with keeping relics of the dead?"

He shuddered dramatically.

"I am sure it will work out for the best," Mr Dunbar continued, attempting a fragile stab at optimism as he pushed open the door to his bedroom. "I have decided that I shall not let it fret me anymore. It will all be just fine. I have told myself this very firmly."

With this positive affirmation, he turned into his room and then he stood stock still, frozen on the spot. Bainbridge, who was a step behind him, could not see past him to note what caused this sudden change in demeanour. But the tension in the man's body informed him that something serious was afoot.

"Mr Dunbar?" he asked, trying to get information from the man.

Mr Dunbar now seemed to tremble like a telegraph wire. Bainbridge put out a hand to touch him and could feel the vibrations. He gently moved the man to one side to try and see what was going on, and it was then that he spied the bed which was in the centre of the room, between two tall windows. It had been freshly made-up that morning with clean linen. Sitting very prominently, one on each of the pair of pillows that dotted the head of the bed were two grinning skulls. They had been positioned very carefully to be facing the observer as they walked in the door. They looked to all intents and purposes, as if someone had placed a skeleton in the bed and the head was resting on the pillow with the rest of the bones beneath the blankets. Bainbridge stared. Mr Dunbar continued to tremble and then he made a gasping sound, and had to grab for a nearby chair to sit down hastily.

Bainbridge walked towards the bed and looked upon the skulls. The mystery had just deepened. It had been logical at first to assume that someone had taken the skulls to destroy Mr Dunbar's, claim on the house. The stealing of the skulls could imply that he had neglected the clauses his aunt had placed in the will, and with the shiftiness of the family lawyer, and the determination of Mr Dunbar's cousin, it would make it easy for the house to fall into different hands. That the skulls were still in the house had also been logical, as they needed to be hidden somewhere. What was not logical, at least from the point of view of Bainbridge's theory, was for the skulls to reappear on Mr

Dunbar's bed.

This changed everything. It felt much more sinister. Something almost like a warning. Bainbridge stepped close to the bed and saw that between the skulls, resting on the cover sheet beneath them, was a note. In large letters that had been carefully drawn out so that you could not identify the handwriting, a message was written.

Who killed us?

Bainbridge stared at the note. Then he looked at the skulls again, thoughtful.

"What does it all mean, Bainbridge?" Dunbar asked from where he was sitting on the chair. "Why have they put these up on my bed? Is it to scare me out of my wits? To haunt me so that I cannot live here?"

"Please, Mr Dunbar, I am trying to think," Bainbridge said, tapping a finger on his chin. "This seems most peculiar. Most peculiar indeed. Who would write such a note when we already have assumed that one of these skulls belonged to Oliver Cromwell and has been here a considerable time, and the other, well, we supposed that was a family member."

"What note?" Dunbar said. Even though he was alarmed, he rose up and peered around Bainbridge's shoulder, curious about this new piece of evidence.

When he spied the note, his eyes widened, and the trembling increased.

"Surely this is to imply that there was a murderer in my family?" he said, before having to sit down again hastily.

"That would certainly be a logical conclusion," Bainbridge confirmed. "Whoever wrote this note is implying that someone murdered these people and kept their skulls, which is in itself a very unpleasant notion. It means that someone was covering up a murder by pretending one of the skulls was that of Oliver Cromwell. As for the other, well, we already know where we found that."

"I am feeling quite queer about all this," Mr Dunbar said. "I think I need to retreat downstairs and maybe get a stiff drink."

"We can at least call off the search," Bainbridge nodded. "But how on earth did these get brought up here?"

"It had to have occurred after I came down and found you," Dunbar said. "Which definitely rules out Jennings, because he has been with your niece all morning."

"That is true," Bainbridge nodded. "It would imply that one of the other servants slipped up here once the search was afoot and placed these skulls when no one was looking. It was done with great care for certain. It also implies that one of your servants knows something about these skulls. Either that or they are playing some terrible hoax, which makes no sense at all. Why would they want to do this to you, Mr Dunbar?"

"I honestly cannot tell you," Mr Dunbar shook his head. "I have never done anything to these people. I have always been kind and nice to them. I kept them on after my aunt died, I told them that they were quite safe and secure here. I cannot see why they would hold a grudge against me."

"If it is not directly against you, and it is not about the house coming to you instead of to your cousin, then maybe it is literally what the note means. Someone here is concerned that two murders have been ignored."

"But Bainbridge, we only found the first skull the other day," Dunbar reminded him. "How could anyone know of it, or the second skull?"

"That in itself is fairly easy to answer," Bainbridge replied. "*You* only discovered the skull the other day, but clearly your aunt knew of it, and presumably your grandfather. Not to mention any of the servants who have been here long enough to have come across it. Many of them have been here for decades, time enough to come across the family secret at some point. The question is, which of them would feel deeply enough about these skulls to want to make a fuss about it?"

"Are you suggesting that there really is some mystery to these skulls? Something more than just people collecting relics? Do you suppose that they really are the heads of murder victims who have been forgotten all this time."

"I am starting to think that is the case," Bainbridge nodded. "Whatever crime is behind them, we must collect them up and take them back downstairs. This mystery is deepening by the moment but if someone has a claim about these skulls and wishes us to determine who they were and who killed them, I would prefer they came forward and admitted it."

"Why would you say that, Bainbridge?"

"Well, it would give us a better opportunity of working out exactly what is going on here. At this moment in time, all we have are two unidentified skulls. If someone came forward and actually said to us this skull belonged to so and so, and he was killed in such-and-such a year, then we would actually have a lead. We might be able to find out who killed them."

"You are supposing someone wants to track down a murderer in my family," Dunbar concluded, catching up slowly. "I am not sure I want to know about a murderer in my family. What a hideous thing to consider."

"I am afraid it is where we are headed with this," Bainbridge told him. "Anyway, let's collect them up and summon Victoria from the servants' quarters. She doesn't need to continue on with her search."

"Should I ring the bell and call up Jennings?" Dunbar said, trying to be helpful.

"Do that," Bainbridge nodded. "Meanwhile, I'm going to see if I can find the box the first skull was in."

Bainbridge did not find the box, so after concluding that there was no other means of bringing them downstairs, he acquired one of Dunbar's old hat boxes. Dunbar was rather squeamish about the fact that one of his best top hats was about to be removed from its box and replaced by a skull, but there was not much else they could do about it, and he did have to admit it was better than contemplating carrying one in his bare hands. The two skulls were placed in the box and carried back downstairs. On the way down, they met with Jennings, who was coming up to see why they had rung for him.

"We have found the skulls, Jennings," Dunbar told him. "And this."

He presented the note to the butler.

Jennings read it, a frown forming on his face.

"Can you think at all what it means?" Dunbar persisted.

"I am sorry, Sir," Jennings said. "But I cannot."

"It means that someone in this household believes the skulls belong to murder victims and want the deaths resolved," Bainbridge told them. "It implies there is a connection between these skulls and someone in the household, some distant family relation, for instance. Because whoever did this, had to have some knowledge about who these skulls belonged to when those persons were alive."

"That is a very curious notion," Jennings said.

"Which of the servants might have done something like this?" Dunbar persisted. "I am not going to say that they are wrong in doing so, and I am not going to be angry about it. I just want to know what is going on here."

"Sir, I honestly do not know."

"Well then," said Bainbridge. "I think it is time we summoned everybody into the drawing room and we got to the bottom of all this. I want to know what's going on here. And if someone wants us to solve the murder of these two skulls, then they have to tell us who they were, because otherwise there is just nothing to go upon."

"I am willing to overlook a great deal in this matter," Dunbar promised. "As long as someone comes forward and explains the truth. I would rather have it all laid out before me then to keep these secrets going."

Jennings nodded his understanding.

"I shall gather everybody, Sir," he agreed. "I wish to get to the bottom of this too, for all our benefits."

Chapter Eighteen

The servants were all gathered together in the drawing room. They looked uneasy, especially as Victoria's search had been suddenly called off. They were all wondering if she had found something. Dunbar, Bainbridge, and Victoria stood in front of the fireplace across from where the servants were massed. Jennings stood with the servants, showing his solidarity with his fellow staff.

Bainbridge was in charge of explanations. He stepped forward, and somewhat dramatically opened the large hat box which had been perched upon a sofa, facing the servants. He revealed the pair of leering skulls. Two of the maids gasped in horror and seemed likely to faint. The third, the youngest, looked on with keen interest. Mrs Moss pressed a handkerchief to her mouth and seemed close to tears, while Jones and Imp stared forward with wonder.

"This whole sorry saga is concerning these two skulls," Bainbridge told the assembled servants. "One of them was found in the attic, in a box that claimed it was the skull of Oliver Cromwell. The other we found in the long lost family vault, where it was mysteriously placed in Matthias Dunbar's coffin. It was these two items that were stolen, and which Victoria was searching for in the servants' quarters. We initially thought they had been stolen as a ploy to ruin Mr Dunbar's reputation, and to make it easier for his cousin to try to claim this house away from him.

"Now it seems there was another reason for the stealing of the skulls, because when we found them this afternoon, there was a note accompanying them."

Bainbridge presented the note to the servants, all of whom, aside from Imp, could read.

"Would you care for me to read it out loud?" Jennings asked.

"Perhaps it would be best," Mr Dunbar said.

Jennings cleared his throat, and in a firm, clear voice, he read.

"Who killed us?"

"Well, that is a rather blunt note," Jones said. "Seems to me quite obvious that someone wants to find out who killed these fellows. What is all this fuss about? Oh, excuse me, Mr Dunbar, I should not speak so brashly, I'm rather used to working alone with the servants."

Jones ducked his head, regretful at his words.

"The point is, Mr Jones," Bainbridge spoke, "that someone in this household clearly believes that here lie two skulls belonging to murder victims. The trouble we have is that we do not know who these people were. These two skulls are as anonymous to us as any in a graveyard."

"We are not here to shout out accusations," Mr Dunbar added. "We would like the person who took these skulls, and then set them in my bedroom, to come forward and explain themselves so that we may do as charged by the note they left."

The servants remained stony silent.

"No one is in trouble. No one will be dismissed for this. We really want to get to the bottom of this mystery. If someone genuinely thinks two persons have been murdered, they must come forward and tell us."

Again, there was nothing from the servants. Dunbar's shoulders slumped. It seemed they were no closer to the solution, and the silence of the culprit meant that further distrust was being spread among his serving staff. He rubbed a hand over his face and looked despondent.

Victoria was the one who stepped forward.

"I am sure we all agreed this is an unpleasant matter, not just the fact that two skulls are being paraded around the house and placed on people's beds, but the fact that these two skulls are here in the first place. If someone knows anything, they must speak up, not just for the sake of everyone here, but for the sakes of these two unfortunates who have been forgotten to history and the crimes against them ignored."

"Once again, I must impress upon you all that I do not blame anyone, and I am not going to dismiss anyone over this matter," Dunbar repeated.

"I am in agreement with the master. I believe it is only right that whoever put these skulls in the bedroom stands up and speaks out," Jennings added.

"I cannot think why anyone would want to touch such things," Mrs Moss declared. "Who would want to touch dead people? It is ghastly. I had no idea that one of these skulls was in the house all these years."

"Mrs Moss, I do not believe you did this," Jennings said to her kindly.

"Well, I am very glad to hear it," Mrs Moss said fiercely. "Because I should never want to be associated with such hideous things. I know of no one being killed in this family, and I have been here many, many years."

"The murders probably occurred long before the current Dunbars lived here," Bainbridge said. "Which also makes it rather peculiar that someone among you knows about them. I assume none of you have family connections to the Dunbar family going back in time?"

"I am afraid, Sir," said Jennings to Bainbridge. "That all of us are rather new here in terms of servants. None of us had a prior ancestor who worked for the family."

"Then are we no further forward," Dunbar said with a sigh. "Am I still to be plagued by this terrible notion that something awful happened in my family, and I know nothing about it? And what of these skulls? What am I to do with them?"

"Perhaps the easiest thing would be to replace them where they came from," Bainbridge told him. "But that is a matter for another time. Right now, we need to decide who among the household raised this concern. We need to know who is behind it, and why they would do such a thing. Otherwise, no one will sleep easy at night. There cannot be distrust among the serving staff in the household. It just will not do."

"On that front, I completely agree," Jennings said, now directing his words to his fellow servants. "We must all speak up and tell the truth. No one is going to be sent away because of this matter, but we must know what is going on."

For a time no one spoke, then Mrs Moss cleared her throat, which was somewhat surprising as no one expected her to confess to the crimes.

"I do not care to point fingers," she said, slightly primly. "But I think if anyone was to do such a thing as this, and perhaps to deem it some terrible joke, I would suggest we look at Imp."

The small man named Imp, who looked more like a child than an adult, startled at this use of his name in connection with the skulls. He was astonished, and that was plain to see.

"Mrs Moss, that is quite unfair. I know I do to have my little jokes, but such a thing as this, is beneath me."

"There is the additional problem," said Jones coming to Imp's defence, "that young Imp here cannot read nor write. He could not have created that note you saw."

"Yet it has to be said, he does play some very silly jokes."

"Not upon the family!" Imp said firmly. "I never would! Never would, Mr Dunbar!"

"All right, Imp," Dunbar held up his hand. "I did not bring you here so that you could start slinging accusations at one another. I hoped that the real perpetrator would step forward and speak up. If nothing else, if they want us to solve this mystery, then we need to know the names of the people the skulls once belonged to."

Still the servants kept their mouths shut, and it seemed they were going to get no further forward. Dunbar finely gave up.

"I think I'm going to contact a new solicitor, someone unconnected to the family, and see if they can advise me on what to do with these skulls," he said. "Maybe there is some way around the matter of having to keep one of them in the house, and a fresh pair of eyes will be able to tell me that."

"It seems a reasonable conclusion," Bainbridge agreed. "As for the second skull, that can be returned to the family vault where it came from. I appreciate you wanted this matter resolved in another way, Mr Dunbar, you wanted to know if you really did have Oliver Cromwell's skull in the house, but I think we need to conclude, for the sake of all our sanities, that the best option is to find a safe home for these skulls and to forget all about them."

Mr Dunbar was in full agreement. He was tired of this matter and its complications.

"This does just leave me one problem," he said to the assembled staff. "Someone among you took these skulls and then placed them on my bed, leaving this note. Had that person come forward and explained themselves, I would have felt much better about it. As it is, I now feel deeply concerned about having you all as my staff. How can I trust you when someone among you did such a thing?"

"Mr Dunbar, Sir. I must impress upon you that all the servants are loyal to you," Jennings said hastily.

"And yet one among them did such a terrible thing," Dunbar shook his head. "I need to think about this long and hard. I gave an opportunity to the culprit to speak up and they refused it. It is hard to know where to go from here. How can a man trust his servants, when they will not be honest with him when he offers them the opportunity to be so?"

"It is surely not as simple as all that," Jennings said, worried that Dunbar might be starting to think about dismissing all the staff again.

"I don't know what to make of it all," Dunbar said. "As I said, I need to think for a while."

He departed the room. Bainbridge glanced at the servants around him.

"I must say I am disappointed as well. I had hoped that someone would step forward, and we could move on with this matter. It is most disagreeable that someone thinks that a murder took place here. But if that person is not prepared to speak up when they are able to, we must simply do as best we can."

He replaced the lid on the hat box.

"You can take dismiss everybody Jennings."

"Yes, Sir," the butler said sadly, turning to his fellow servants and shuffling them out the door. No one said a word.

"Well, that did not go as planned," Victoria groaned to Bainbridge.

"Didn't it?" Bainbridge grinned at her.

Chapter Nineteen

V ictoria and Bainbridge retired to the library, there to await what would come next. Bainbridge seemed certain that something would come of their strange conversation in the drawing room with the servants. Victoria was not as convinced, though she had to admit her uncle had his ways about him, and maybe he had picked up something that she had not. In any case, with little else to go on, they decided to sit and sift through some more family documents, to see if there was any clue as to where the skulls had come from originally.

"There will be a logic to this somewhere," Bainbridge said to his niece. "There must be some clue amongst all this stuff that will tell us why the skulls are here and why someone would suppose they belonged to murder victims."

"I don't quite have your confidence," Victoria responded. "I think we are at a dead end, and probably the best thing to do would be to speak to the local vicar and have the skulls discreetly buried."

"That is very probably the way we will end up going," Bainbridge nodded. "After all, what else is there to do for the poor victims? I do wonder where the rest of their bodies are. I mean, if one had been the head of Oliver Cromwell, we would know what had become of his body. But now we have two unidentified skulls. Somewhere around here there must be some corpses to go with them."

"That is altogether a very grim thought," Victoria remarked.

She gave a little shudder as she had visions that deep beneath the cellar floors there might be some hidden corpses.

"Do not think about it too hard," Bainbridge told her. "I am sure that this is all linked to some quite banal family mystery."

"Such as?" Victoria asked.

"Well, that is the dilemma. What precisely might have resulted in them being brought away from their bodies and kept in boxes and the family vault? We might assume that they had once belonged to family members, and that for some reason they had been deposited outside of their regular coffins."

"Which in itself is rather unpleasant," Victoria went to a shelf and took down some more papers she had noted the day before. These ones were from the eighteenth century, and though they were later than they supposed the skulls had been buried, it seemed just as feasible to look for clues there as it did in the older papers, which had proved uninspiring so far.

"My point is, having a skull in the house does not mean that something malicious occurred. Though it could mean that as well, I suppose. It depends on how fresh the skull is, whether the occupants of the house knew it was there or not, and all manner of other stuff. In fact, now I come to think of it, I have had quite a few cases where skulls have been found in homes and it has proven to be murder, so perhaps I am mistaken in that as well."

Victoria shook her head at her uncle's ramblings.

"Well, you seem convinced that someone is going to give us some information that will enlighten us."

"I am," Bainbridge promised her. "I saw it in the faces of the servants. Someone definitely knows something, and I have given them an opportunity to speak out."

"I saw you give no opportunity," Victoria said.

"Ah, but that was because the opportunity was subtle. Speaking before all the fellow servants was clearly too much for the culprit. I knew that would probably be the case. The reason we brought them all together was to enable us to tell everyone all at once what we were thinking and what was going on, and to mention the threat about the servants being distrusted, and maybe even being dismissed. This, to my mind, will prick the conscience of our culprit, and they will respond in due course. They simply could not speak out in front of everyone else."

"You are placing a lot of hope on someone's conscience," Victoria remarked.

"I find that a person's conscience is usually their most reliable trait," Bainbridge opened an old volume, which proved to be full of family recipes and medicinal potions. He started flicking through it out of curiosity more than anything. Half of the text was old wives' tales and folk remedies. The sort of things that were half magic, half genuine. Most of them would have been ineffective.

"I would like to suppose..." Victoria began to speak when suddenly they heard a knock on the door.

They both turned to the library door and, as they did so, they saw something being shoved underneath it. It was a note. Victoria hastened to the door, but by the time she got there whoever had knocked was gone. All that was left was the note, which she carried back to the table.

"Aha, the plot thickens," Bainbridge said confidently. "I knew my ploy would get a result."

Victoria opened the note, which had been folded in half.

"It appears that whoever is concerned about the skulls, has given us some information," she said. "It reads thus, 'if you would like to determine the truth behind the skulls, and it would please me deeply if you did, then I suggest you look for volume ten of the late Miss Dunbar's personal diaries. You shall find it on the shelves where the family papers are kept. Third row up, close to a volume of poems.'"

Bainbridge quickly headed to the shelf and, using the directions supplied in the note, he soon spied the book, which as had been stated, was numbered volume ten. Miss Dunbar had been quite the diarist. She had kept diaries all her life, and each one was carefully numbered. Volume ten appeared to have been written when she was in her early twenties. He brought it to the table.

"I don't suppose they gave us any further clue than that?"

"No, I am afraid they did not," Victoria said. "And the writing is once again printed in a hand that makes it difficult to recognise."

"Difficult, but maybe not impossible," Bainbridge said, then he flipped open the diary.

"This is quite a weighty tome," he said, looking at the number of pages and the small script which Miss Dunbar had written in.

She had not written in the diary every single day, and the volume spanned over at least three years. Bainbridge settled down to read it, and they all fell into quiet thought. Victoria went through more family papers, and came across some old plans that had been carelessly folded up into a book of household accounts. When she unfolded the plans gingerly, because they were papery thin and looked ready to fall apart, she realised that she was looking at the original plans for the family vault. She spotted the date and the name of the architect who designed them. Then she studied them. Yes, here it was – the big square vault, room enough for the six coffins, the ornamentation, the steps leading down, and even notes about where it would be located in the grounds.

"I may have something," Bainbridge said, distracting her from the plans.

Victoria glanced over.

"What is it?"

"Here, dated the 10th of July 1834, Miss Dunbar records that she came across a strange document in the library while she was researching the family history. She says this document recorded a curious family legend but she does not speak of it further, other than to say it involved two Dunbar sisters. They were unmarried, much like herself, and they had a strong devotion to the house. Something happened to them and there seems to be some mystery about their burial."

"Depending on the date, they could have been buried in the family vault," Victoria said.

"This would have been after that," Bainbridge said, tapping the page. "But Miss Dunbar has not added more at this stage. I shall keep reading. Maybe we have more here."

"Do you think the two skulls are connected to the family legend?"

"They could be. After all, we have this talk of a mysterious burial and two anonymous skulls. I wish I was clever enough to work out if the skulls were male or female, I hear tell that is possible."

Victoria thought about the two skulls they had seen. The glaring eye sockets, the grim teeth. She could not see how either of them could be described as feminine. She had assumed they were both male.

"If this is the clue to the skulls and why someone says they were murdered, then there must be more to it," she said.

"I have it!" Bainbridge declared in delight as his finger was following along the lines of writing on the page. "Yes, Miss Dunbar wrote further on the matter. She determined that there was a family legend that the two sisters had been murdered at a young age – they would only have been in their twenties, as she was when she was researching them. The family legend went as follows, the incident occurred at the time that the Georgian wing was being added to the house. This project had been initiated by the two sisters, who at this time lived here with their father. They were devoted to the project. They were constantly checking the plans and watching the progress and were determined to see it through.

"Then something terrible happened, this mysterious incident, and both of them succumbed. Now they did not die at once from whatever struck them, but they lingered and upon their deathbeds, they both insisted that they should not be buried outside the house. They wanted to be buried within the Georgian wing so that they could always be close to the project they had started."

"Well, that is perfectly horrible," Victoria shivered.

"It may be to us, but clearly not to them," Bainbridge continued. "Of course, the family initially decided that the two sisters must be buried in the local graveyard, and that was what was done. Then mysterious things began to occur, incidents about the house that people ascribed to ghostly activity. You know the sort of thing, a door slams and everybody is up in arms.

"Well, the family decided it must be the sisters playing up and pointing out that their death wishes had not been fulfilled. So the bodies were exhumed, would you believe, and the heads removed and brought into the Georgian wing, where they were then placed under the floorboards of the drawing room."

"That would be the new drawing room," Victoria pointed out. "Not the old dining room where we had the skulls originally."

"Exactly, anyway, the skulls were brought inside, placed beneath the floor, and everything seemed quiet after that. Which would seem to be the end of the mystery, except – and this is the interesting bit – Miss Dunbar decided to have the floor lifted up. She persuaded her father that it must be done as there could be a rat problem, when really she was curious about whether these skulls were there, and lo and behold, when the floor was lifted, the skulls were missing."

"The reasonable thing would be to suppose the story was untrue."

"Absolutely, and that is what I would have thought. But Miss Dunbar must have been intrigued by this legend, and refused to leave it alone. She mentions here that she intends to follow up on her research. All of which would be academic, aside from the fact that there are now two skulls in the house."

"Two skulls only because we brought the second one here from the family vault."

"Exactly. It had been hidden," Bainbridge said. "And now here we have this story. Why I think it might be possible to identify these skulls after all."

"Even so, it still leaves us with two significant questions," Victoria pointed out. "Firstly, who is the person who knows about these murders and is playing silly games with us? And secondly, who killed the women in the first place?"

"I think that is the key to all this," Bainbridge wagged a finger at her. "We solve that mystery and all of Mr Dunbar's troubles may just disappear."

Chapter Twenty

Since they were aware Mr Dunbar knew little about his family history there seemed no point asking him about the murdered spinster sisters. They decided to continue to explore the library shelves in the hope there may be some clue among the many papers. They swiftly found documents relating to the eighteenth century, and specifically to the building of the Georgian wing. Like all old houses, the Dunbars' house had been expanded and added to by various generations who wanted to make their mark on the property. There were plans for everything, from different wings and rooms, to additions to the roof, some of which had never been built. There were curious drawings for gargoyles that had once been considered during the Gothic Victorian revival, and for a peculiar cupola that was supposed to house a clock, and which one former Dunbar had thought would make a stylish addition to the home. Letters revealed that there had been concerns that the roof structure would not support the weight and that, despite this, vain attempts had been made to put it up with the expected result. It had blown down one stormy night and shattered on the courtyard flagstones, disturbing one of the resident cats, and upsetting one of the ladies of the house so greatly that she refused to ever go beyond the ground floor again.

They slowly worked through all these old documents until they came across the one they wanted. This was the original architectural plans for the Georgian wing. They spied the name of the architect at the bottom, but it gave no clue as to who had commissioned it.

"We must cross reference this with the family tree in the family Bible," Bainbridge said and hastened to find this weighty tome.

There were, in fact, several family Bibles on the shelves of the Dunbar library. All of them were sizable; considerably bigger than any regular book. One of them was so gargantuan that it was almost impossible to lift off the shelf. Bainbridge struggled with the cargo, getting it so far and then wondering if he was going to tumble over under the awkward weight. Victoria had to rush to his aid. It took both of them to get the book onto the table. The Bible was at least three feet in height and at least one and a half feet in width. This monstrous volume, grand as it was, would have been impossible to read easily except at a table, and even then it would require the reader to lean uncomfortably forward.

It had been made as a status symbol rather than to be an actual book. Bainbridge shook his head looking at it. He always fancied that a book was a practical item, that it should be for reading. When it became an ornamental thing to just be housed on the shelf and look grand, to display the family's wealth and prestige, he felt it had lost something of its purpose. However, the size of the giant Bible meant that there was plenty of room for an extensive family tree on the front page, and it did not take long, as they read through the names, for them to work out which family members the old legend must refer to. Two Dunbar ladies were born in 1701 and 1705, respectively. One was named Eliza and the other Alice. Alice and Eliza had never married according to the family Bible and, interestingly, they had both died in the same year which was 1729.

There was nothing to indicate what had caused the sudden deaths of the two sisters, but it certainly was curious, and it tied in with the construction of the Georgian wing, which had begun in 1725. Most such large projects took time and would be completed over several years. Occasionally, it was to do with how finances waxed and waned within the family, or how and when workmen were available. Still, it was logical that these were the two sisters connected to the construction of this particular wing.

The question was how did they find out more about Eliza and Alice? Bainbridge tapped his chin thoughtfully.

"You know," Victoria said. "We could go to the graveyard and see if they have tombstones."

Bainbridge shook his head.

"That would hardly help us because we know from the family legend they were buried in the graveyard and *then* their heads were exhumed at a later date. The graves should still be there with their bodies in them."

Victoria felt her skin crawl at this notion, but she aimed not to say anything. She had to get better at this 'being around the dead' lark. It was par for the course for being a private detective. For someone who was endeavouring to solve the sudden and unexpected deaths of people as part of their daily work, she needed to get a bit tougher with herself when it came to corpses and her reaction to them.

"Let us concern ourselves with finding family papers relating to this period of time," Bainbridge decided. "Among them, there may be a clue."

They looked to the shelves, which, it had to be said, were somewhat disorganised. No one had ever spent time cataloguing the family documents. Mr Dunbar's aunt had shown some interest in them, yet it had clearly not extended to cataloguing what was there, and arranging everything at least by date. Everything was in a different place. There were documents from the start of the house construction muddled in with records concerning expenses for the garden a few years back. They both studied the scene before them.

"Well, there is only one thing for it," Bainbridge said firmly. "You start that end, I'll start this."

They spent over an hour sorting through documents, trying to find those that related to Eliza and Alice. It didn't help that some of the papers they found were not dated, causing further consternation. They ended up with a pile of documents that stemmed from account books to another one of those recipe books which included family potions. They came across a folder which contained letters, another that contained drawings made by one of the former Dunbars of the house. Then Bainbridge turned up an old will. He was slightly concerned that this was in the possession of the family and not with their solicitors.

He examined it very closely, reading through it over and over, until Victoria got frustrated with him.

"I do not see that will has anything to do with what we are dealing with here," she told him. "You have been examining it for at least ten minutes."

Bainbridge paused and looked up.

"I need to read this very carefully," he said. "Just in case. There is something niggling at the back of my mind over it. I cannot tell you just what, and the writing is archaic. But if I can just dig deep enough into it..."

"It is not relevant for the case before us," Victoria pointed out to him gently.

"Yes, yes, well wills are always curious things and it shouldn't be here. It should be safely with the family solicitor. I shall put it to one side and look at it another time."

They went back to the papers before them and with plenty of patience, they started to uncover documents that related to Eliza and Alice. Thus they came across a book that had been compiled by Alice and appeared to contain details of the family project on the Georgian wing. The story they had heard was clearly true that Alice and Eliza were the instigators behind the new structure. Alice wrote in her diary that she and her sister had been charged by their father to oversee the work. He had felt it was a good project for them, the Dunbar male line generally being quite keen to encourage their daughters just as they would encourage their sons. Many a family would not have taken interest in two girls wanting to involve themselves in the construction of a new wing. They would think it unseemly for women. But the Dunbar men had been of a different calibre. Just like the most recent elder Mr Dunbar who had encouraged his daughter to be his assistant.

Alice was clearly an intelligent girl and she kept a close eye on the expenditure of money for materials used in the new wing. She was good at overseeing the construction and keeping a thorough eye on the accounts. Having seen this, Bainbridge and Victoria were certain that at least part of the legend was true, and that the girl would have been devastated to have not seen the completion of the wing she had taken such pride in. Alice's diary stopped rather suddenly halfway through the book, leaving many empty pages. The date was the 17th of August 1729. The year she had passed away, along with her sister. The curiosity of the timing piqued Bainbridge's interest.

"We need to dig into this further. What else can we find about this Miss Dunbar?"

They kept looking, but the papers were starting to become fruitless. There were letters, but they didn't seem to relate to the particular sisters, and they could find nothing else that would indicate what had happened to them. After exploring the documents for over an hour, they started to feel despondent.

"There is nothing else here," Victoria sighed. "All I see is volume after volume about family accounts and special recipes for getting rid of coughs."

"I do confess the Dunbars seemed to have been particularly afflicted by coughs if you go by the number of recipes they collected for curing them," Bainbridge nodded. "But it is unhelpful for us regarding Eliza and Alice."

"Then what do we do next?" Victoria asked.

"We do what I always do," Bainbridge said. "We widen the field of interest. If there are no documents here within the family collection, then we need to go to other places. I would suggest speaking to the family solicitor, but at this point I don't want him knowing what we are up to."

"Then what are these other places you refer to?" Victoria asked.

"Well, that really does depend. We could always go to the police and ask them about their records, because if the sisters were murdered, as is claimed, there should be some record concerning it. Not that there was an actual police force back then, but there should be court records and something from whoever was in charge of looking into the matter."

"But the family legend stated that nobody was ever charged for killing them," Victoria pointed out.

"In which case," Bainbridge said, "We find ourselves in a difficult position. In 1729, we won't have much luck from newspaper articles either."

Victoria shook her head.

"You know, I think we are just back at a dead end."

"No, there has to be something more we can do," Bainbridge said firmly. "We just have to keep looking. Maybe there is somewhere else where records for the family were kept."

They both turned to look at the disorganised shelves. They were fairly confident they had scoured them thoroughly and found everything that was there.

"You know there is one other place," Victoria said and she nodded her head upwards.

"Now that is a good point," Bainbridge said. "We supposed that Mr Dunbar's aunt had specified in her will that nothing must be removed from the attic because of the skull. I wonder if that is not the case and, actually, there is something up there that would point towards the killer of Eliza and Alice."

"If there were more, wouldn't Miss Dunbar have taken it up herself in her lifetime?" Victoria asked.

"Maybe she was not able to, or maybe she felt she was not in a position to do so. Don't forget she was a spinster lady living alone in this property. Perhaps she didn't feel she would be taken seriously if she did something like that. In any case, we ought to look. There must be something more here, something we have missed."

"And if we find nothing upstairs?" Victoria asked.

Bainbridge was stoic.

"We cross that bridge when we come to it," he said. "I am not done yet, Vicky. Far from it."

Chapter Twenty-One

They walked up to the attic. Bainbridge grumbled at the number of stairs he had been forced to navigate over the last few days; he preferred his cases to revolve mainly around ground floor rooms. He felt the strain in his knees and in his back, and he resolved that he wasn't quite as recovered from his adventure to the family vault as he had supposed.

Victoria glanced back at him once or twice. The look of concern on her face worried him – did he really give the appearance of being so unhealthy? He caught his breath and tried to console himself with his usual self-deception. His difficulty with the stairs had nothing to do with his health or his weight, it was to do with the fact they had made stairs so steep in the past. How was anyone supposed to climb such stairs in a dignified manner and without losing their breath?

Satisfied that he had explained to himself what was going on with his body, and that it had nothing to do with his own gargantuan appetite, or that he potentially needed to do something about his lifestyle, he carried on upwards.

In the attic he perched for a moment on an old chair that creaked worryingly under his weight. Victoria cast another look in his direction and he had wagged a finger at her.

"None of that. I am tired of your glances. I am perfectly fine."

"Is it not the remit of a niece to worry about her uncle?" Victoria said.

"You may worry. Just don't cast those accusing glances at me."

"If you perhaps just consented to the diet I suggested..."

Victoria bit her tongue when she saw the darkening expression on her uncle's face. There were some battles you just could not win.

"Fine, then drop dead on one of your cases. See if I care," she snapped.

She was angry because she was worried about him.

Bainbridge was hurt but he was not going to admit defeat. There was no way he was going to consent to being put on a diet. Such a thing he considered to be a death before death.

A difficult silence fell between them. Bainbridge, somewhat recovered from his exertions, rose from the chair.

"Well, I suppose we ought to look around for places where you might hide documents," he suggested.

His gentle tone was an attempt to build bridges with Victoria and to mollify her.

She sighed.

"I care about you. Is that so bad?"

"It is a very pleasant thing indeed," Bainbridge told her. "But there is only so much caring a person can take."

Victoria nodded her understanding and they set to work. There was an awful lot of stuff in the attic; the collective detritus of many generations, things that should have been thrown away and that weren't. Mouldering teddy bears, gowns that had been decimated by moths, items of furniture that should have made it onto the bonfire long ago. Families such as the Dunbars became hoarders because they had the space for it. So much junk had been holed up in the loft that it would easily fill a pawn shop with stock to spare.

They found trunks of belongings labelled with the names of long dead family members. When a Dunbar died, any of their belongings that were not going to be kept in the house, were bundled up, put away carefully in a trunk, and then set in the attic for some future generation to come across and ponder over.

There was a trunk that contained a riding whip, and a pair of men shoes along with some old coins.

Another was filled with more of the art books that Bainbridge had come across in the library. It turned out that at least one of the Dunbar family had been a very keen artist, and had filled book after book with drawings. Some of them were even quite good.

"This is going to take a long time," Victoria said starting to regret her idea.

"I agree," Bainbridge replied. "We could do with an extra pair of hands or two. I suggest we summon up Mr Dunbar, and we ask that Jennings prepares refreshments for us and then joins us here. Between the four of us, we shall make short work of it all."

It seemed a very reasonable idea, so Victoria headed back downstairs and rang for Jennings. He appeared swiftly and she explained what they were up to. He promised to go get a tray of refreshments and to inform his master that they were in the attic and needed assistance.

It was around half an hour later that Mr Dunbar turned up in the attic and looked around him. The glances he gave at all the various boxes and dusty corners told them that he was worrying that another skull might suddenly appear before him. He had already had one fright when searching the attic for old belongings, he was not inclined to have another. Bainbridge waved him in.

"Come along man, we may just have the solution before us, but you have to assist us."

"What precisely do you want me to do?" Dunbar asked, staring in distaste at the hoarded rubbish.

"We need to look for any information concerning a Miss Eliza Dunbar and a Miss Alice Dunbar," Bainbridge explained.

Dunbar raised an eyebrow in surprise.

"Oh well, I know all about them."

Victoria and Bainbridge came to a halt in their searches and paused to look at him.

"What do you mean you know all about them?" Victoria asked him sternly.

"My aunt told me all about them," Dunbar explained. "They were quite a passion of hers, you see. She had researched the family tree quite a long way back, and she had come across these two girls, Eliza and Alice. Once she knew their names, she became fascinated with them. Do you know it was said they were both murdered and Alice asked for her head to be buried beneath the floor of the drawing room? Though my aunt assured me that there were no heads there, for she had it checked herself."

Bainbridge ran a hand over his face, wondering when the poor fool might have realised that the two skulls that they were dealing with were related to the two skulls he had been told about. Dunbar was looking at them keenly, completely oblivious to the fact that he had wasted a good deal of their time, and that if he had just mentioned this whole story in the first place, they might have resolved this case by now.

"Did you not think to mention this story to us?" Victoria spoke their thoughts.

Dunbar looked genuinely surprised at the comment.

"Why would I do a thing like that?" He said. "It was only an old family legend and there is no truth to it because there were no skulls."

"There were no skulls beneath the drawing room floor," Bainbridge pointed out. "There *was* a skull up here, in the attic, of mysterious origins, and then we found a second one in the family vault. I can understand that *maybe* when the first one cropped up you didn't connect it with the story of Eliza and Alice, but what about when the second one appeared?"

Dunbar looked dumbfounded.

"Oh," he said as the realisation sunk into him. "You make quite the point, yes. I never really connected it."

"What did your aunt tell you about these two girls, in any case?" Bainbridge asked, deciding there was no point haranguing the man about the fact that he had, all along, known the possible answer to the mystery of the skulls.

"Well, she had done some considerable research on them," Dunbar explained, hastening to be helpful now. "She had heard the family legend, but it was rather vague, so she looked into matters further. She went to the local graveyard, and she found the girls' gravestones. They had died within a day of each other, so that added weight to the story, but it could have just been that they died of some illness. There were plenty of those to go around in the past.

"Then she began to make inquiries. You have to remember that when she was doing this, it was around the 1830s and the girls had died in the 1720s, just over 100 years back. Which meant that though there was no one alive who knew them in living memory, she was able to find a few people who had been told the story by their grandparents or parents. She pieced together the whole sorry affair from what they told her.

"Apparently, Eliza had a secret lover. Someone who her parents would not have approved of because of his circumstances. She hoped to elope with him but her sister, Alice, discovered the story, and was so upset to think that her sister might abandon her, that she said she would tell their parents unless Eliza broke off the engagement. Eliza told her young man, and he took matters into his own hands. He had an argument with Alice in which she was thrown down the stairs and hit her head.

"It was hoped that she might survive the ordeal, but really it was a vain idea. The injury was too great, and she lingered for only a matter of days before dying. However, in that time she told her sister what had occurred. She would not reveal the name of the young man to their parents out of love for her sister, but Eliza knew the truth. Eliza could not bear to think that she had been the cause of her beloved sister's death. So, she took her own life using poison, that she could follow Alice to the grave.

"She wrote one last letter before she died explaining why she had done it, and she left this for her parents to see. But out of some misplaced loyalty to the young man who had killed her sister she did not name him. She asked that no one pursue the matter any further, and that they allow the sisters to rest in peace together. Then, of course, there was the strange story about the Alice wanting her skull to be buried beneath the drawing room.

"My aunt told me that Alice had written a final letter on her death bed. She had named the culprit who had killed her, and she had advised that if she were to die from her injuries, he should be named, so that her sister would not marry him. After all, who would want their sister to marry a murderer?

"However, this letter vanished immediately after Alice died. My aunt believed that Eliza had taken it and hidden it somewhere to prevent her betrothed being uncovered as a murderer."

"And how did your aunt find out about the matter?" Bainbridge asked.

"From the daughter of a former servant of the family who remembered that her mother had told her all about it. Her mother had nursed poor Alice during her final days. She had also been told about a ghost story connected to the girls. When Alice died, her final request that her head was buried beneath the drawing room floor was ignored, as was only logical. No doubt the request was felt to have been made due to the delirium she suffered at the end of her days.

"However, a short time after the funeral, strange things began to happen in the house. Knocks, bangs, even some shrieks as if a person was falling down the stairs. Terrified it was the vengeful spirit of Alice, her deathbed request was at last performed and her skull placed beneath the drawing room floor. Of course, it was all nonsense as there was no skull when my aunt looked for it."

Mr Dunbar paused.

"Alice's skull was up here, all along," he looked dazed by the revelation.

"Then the message we received was true," Victoria said to her uncle. "Alice was murdered, and someone wants justice for her, and for Eliza who was broken by her own guilt. They want us to reveal who did it so that at last Alice and Eliza can have some peace."

"You never mentioned this before," Bainbridge said crossly to Dunbar.

Dunbar merely shrugged.

"I believe I said that I didn't think there were any murderers in my family, which is absolutely true. The person was not one of my family, and never became one of my family. So there you have it. In any case until a few moments ago, I didn't really think the story was true. I must admit I am feeling very confused."

Dunbar sat down heavily in one of the old chairs that was in the attic. It was at that moment the old chair decided to give up the ghost and collapsed down to the ground in a cloud of dust and dead insects. All they could hear for several moments was Dunbar coughing and spluttering. When the dust settled, he looked as though he was auditioning for the part of the household ghost.

"Oh dear," Victoria tried not to chuckle as she went to his aid.

Dunbar scowled.

"I hate this attic," he stated emphatically.

Chapter
Twenty-Two

By the time Jennings arrived at the attic, they had managed to dust off Mr Dunbar, so he didn't look quite so much like the spectre from Oscar Wilde's *The Canterville Ghost*. Jennings still gave his master a curious look when he arrived in the room.

"An old chair disagreed with me," Dunbar said, feeling he needed to explain himself to his butler.

Jennings was an old master at not showing his feelings around his superiors, and so he did nothing more except place the tray of refreshments down on a handy table and come forward with a handkerchief to wipe off Mr Dunbar's face.

"We are looking for a missing letter," Bainbridge told the butler now he was present. "It was written by Alice Dunbar around 1729. It contains details of the man who killed her by pushing her down the stairs."

Jennings raised an eyebrow because that statement did not sound entirely logical.

"She didn't die at once," Victoria added. "She hit her head and lingered, so she was able to write the letter. I suppose there was swelling on the brain or something like that."

"Something along those lines," Bainbridge nodded. "Head injuries can be tricky beggars. I have seen a few in the army. Some you would never suppose a man could recover from, and others would look quite minor but took the fellow away from this world in a matter of days."

"Well, whatever happened to poor Miss Alice we need to find that letter and resolve some part of this mystery. Once we know who killed her, then we can safely bury the skulls, and hopefully all this matter will be sorted out," Victoria said to them all.

Dunbar was looking brighter at this news.

"I will gladly help you," he said.

"I think the first thing to do is to search this entire attic from top to bottom," Bainbridge declared. "That way we can be certain that the letter is not hidden here somewhere. I suspect it is not, because if I was Miss Eliza, I would have made sure to hide it somewhere no one could ever get their hands on it."

"May I say, Sir, in a house as big as this, that offers a lot of potential places for it to be hidden," Jennings said sadly.

"That is very true," Dunbar now lost his smile. "My aunt must have looked thoroughly about the house for it. I cannot believe she wouldn't have."

"We just have to keep trying," Bainbridge said. "Unless it was totally destroyed, it has to be around here somewhere."

"I hadn't thought of that," Dunbar's expression turned to a frown. "Yes. What if she burned it?"

"That will all depend on just how far Eliza was prepared to go for her lover," Victoria remarked. "She may not have wished to see him condemned in her lifetime, that does not mean she wanted his crimes to be forgotten forever."

"Let us hope she decided to hide the letter rather than destroy it," Bainbridge said. "In which case, we need to get on with this business for it is nearly evening again and we are no further forward."

"Sir, did anything come from the meeting we held with the servants?" Jennings asked.

"It achieved what I expected it to achieve," Bainbridge explained. "We received a note not long after. Anonymous, of course, but it gave us the clue we needed to find ourselves up here. Now we are closer to the truth. We know that our skulls most likely are those of Eliza and Alice Dunbar, who both died in the year 1729 as a consequence of the actions of Eliza's fiancé. If we can just determine who that man was, we can bring justice for those girls."

Jennings nodded his head in understanding.

"Then may I suggest we divide ourselves equally about the attic, and do our best to cover as much ground as possible," he said.

"It sounds a wise notion," Bainbridge agreed. "Victoria and myself will go down the lower end, closest to where the skull was found, to relieve Mr Dunbar of any worries that there might be further mysterious body parts hidden about that he could stumble across. You two can remain up this end."

Dunbar was more than agreeable to this notion and happily picked himself a spot near a small window that allowed in a minimum amount of light to the old attic. Victoria and Bainbridge headed down the other end. They were soon immersed in digging through old boxes, scrounging around ancient dresses, jackets, forgotten children's toys, ornaments that should have been thrown out but had sentimental value and so had to remain, and everything else that a family acquires but cannot quite get rid of.

Victoria came across an interesting trunk that was covered in white calfskin rather than the grey or black that was everywhere else. It had pretty pale brown straps and corner protectors and it looked like something a lady would use. She thought it was rather handsome and could imagine owning it herself. She was intrigued to discover what might be inside. When she lifted the lid, her heart sank a fraction. Inside was a dress; a gown designed in the style of the Georgian period and, from the looks of it, and the way it had been carefully detailed with lace, she could guess that it had meant to be a wedding dress. There was a cap with a veil, and when she dug deeper, she found a pair of shoes. They were not white but dove grey. It was only in the Victorian age that people had begun to feel that the bride should walk to the altar dressed all in white – a symbolic action supposed to indicate her purity.

Prior to then, people wore whatever colour they chose to their wedding, and had whatever nice dress they fancied. This one was a pale green with tiny details of flowers all across the surface. She touched the cloth and felt how soft it was beneath her fingers. The dress was pristine. It had never been worn. She stared inside the trunk. She had a hunch who this had meant to be for. After a while, she lifted it out of the box and looked to see what was beneath it. She found a book which contained pressed flowers and poems. The frontispiece indicated that this book had been the property of Eliza Dunbar. She started to get more items out of the trunk. These were the relics of a girl who had died too young. Even if her parents did not know about her secret lover, it was no surprise that Eliza had a dress specially made for when she eloped.

Victoria recalled that once, not so long ago, she had been the same. That there was a dress still sitting in her wardrobe at home. It had been ready for her ill-fated marriage to Sven. She was glad, after all, that she had not married him, and marriage was now a distant thought. She was far too interested in being an independent woman, and marriage would steal that from her. Even so, she could feel sadness for a girl's dreams that had been torn apart due to one tragic mishap.

She drew out several books from the trunk. Eliza had been a keen writer. She didn't have journals like her sister or Mr Dunbar's aunt, but she did like to create poems and fill book after book with them. She did little sketches to accompany them. She made notes of places they had been to, dances they had attended and who she had danced with and other such things. Victoria fancied that hidden among all these little items, there could be a clue as to who might have been her secret lover. So she gathered up all the books and set them to one side. The remainder of the items in the box were personal items; pieces of jewellery, a hair comb, a forlorn doll that had been loved nearly to pieces, and repaired many times. All the small relics of a life packed up into one trunk.

She was nearly finished with the trunk and thought she had seen everything that needed to be seen, when something else caught her eye. There was a small box almost hidden at one corner. When she fumbled it out in the darkness, she saw that it was covered in dove grey velvet. When she opened it, she found it contained a ring. It had to be an engagement ring. She studied it for a while.

"Julius, you ought to come see this," she called over her shoulder.

Her uncle walked across the attic to see what she had found. She presented him with the ring.

"These are all the belongings of Eliza Dunbar," she explained. "Here is her wedding gown, her wedding shoes, her wedding veil, all the things she had planned to use and all the things she never had the chance to wear. There are books with poems inside and notes. There may be something in them. She kept a list of who she danced with. You never know, it could be a clue."

Bainbridge was looking at the ring. Sadness had come over him as well. The story of the sisters' unfortunate demise had hit him hard. It had been so tragic and unnecessary, he thought, and all due to the fact that a family could not bear for Eliza to marry someone they deemed beneath her. Then again, it could be argued that a man who pushed someone down the stairs was not someone you would wish your daughter to marry anyway.

"We need to take all these things back downstairs and go through them thoroughly," he said. "But keep looking, there might be more here that we have yet to find."

"How did it all happen, do you suppose?" Victoria said, staring at the items around her. "How did the two girls' heads end up like this? One being called that of Oliver Cromwell's and the other in a family vault."

"Odd things happen over the centuries," Bainbridge shrugged. "People's memories are shorter than we realise. Within a generation much can be forgotten and lost."

"That does not really explain it at all," Victoria scolded him.

At that moment, there was a shout from the other end of the attic.

"Look what I found," cried out Mr Dunbar. "I might have something of an answer."

Chapter Twenty-Three

D unbar's elation came from holding up a letter that he had discovered among a collection of similar missives in one of the many boxes. The letter had been written from an antiquities dealer sometime in the early 1800s. This antiquities dealer had been summoned to the house by one of the Dunbar menfolk, and had been asked to look at a skull that had been found recently beneath the drawing room floor.

"You see, not long after the completion of the Georgian wing, according to the letters that I found along with this one, there was a problem. There seemed to be an excessive amount of damp in the room, and the floor appeared to be buckling. So the boards were taken up in a specific place and beneath it they found a skull," Dunbar elaborated. "It quite shocked the family at the time. This would have been during my great grandfather's period at the house. I say this in a delicate way, but he was perhaps more like me than the others. From what my aunt has told me, her grandfather was somewhat sensitive and reminded her a great deal of me.

"When he discovered the skull beneath the floorboards, he was quite upset. I suppose anybody would be, really. None of the family at the time seemed to know why it was there or of the family legend.

"Certainly no one mentioned that this was probably the skull of either Eliza or Alice, and my great grandfather was left to his own devices to try and figure it all out. He determined to get an expert in, someone who could look at the skull and determine where it had come from. He also had this idea in his head that it might have been the head of Oliver Cromwell.

"Reading between the lines of these letters, it would seem that my great grandfather was fascinated by the English Civil War and had read how Oliver Cromwell's head had been displaced from its pike and hidden somewhere. It turns out our family were quite the parliamentarians during the Civil War, and he was hopeful that the head beneath the floorboards was that of Oliver Cromwell, who was something of a hero to him. You can understand why he might be inspired by such a man, and we are not so far from the home of Oliver Cromwell after all."

"Oliver Cromwell lived in Ely," Bainbridge nodded. "Yes, I suppose you could argue that there was a relatively close tie."

"My uncle sent for this expert in antiquities, a gentleman all the way from Edinburgh," Dunbar continued with his story. "The man knew all about skulls and also the story of Oliver Cromwell. He came down, and he wrote a letter certifying that, to the best of his knowledge, the skull that had been found must be that of Oliver Cromwell and should be treated with due respect. He also said it was a valuable item and needed to be kept very secure. I think we can now see how the skull ended up in a box here in the attic."

"Sir, if I may, there are further letters here and they appear to be invoices for work to make a lead box that would have been suitable for placing up here in the attic," Jennings said.

"Well, there you have it. At least we know how one skull ended up being called that of Oliver Cromwell," Victoria said, crossing her arms. "It is just a pity that we don't know how the other skull ended up in the family vault nor who killed them."

"Is it not remarkable that so soon after the family tragedy, such an incident as this could occur?" Dunbar remarked. "We are talking about, what? Just over seventy years. Yet, apparently, my great grandfather had no knowledge of the two unfortunate sisters."

"You said yourself, the family considered your great grandfather a delicate soul. If we looked at the family tree, I suppose he would have been the grandson of whoever was in the house at the time of Eliza and Alice's demise. If we suppose the family wanted to keep the matter of the girls' deaths relatively quiet, then it would make sense that he was never told about them. Such secrets within families can disappear without a trace."

"I am thinking of it this way," Victoria added. "Alice made this strange request to be buried beneath the drawing room floor, and this was upsetting for the family. Of course, at first they did not bother to do it. They could not face such a thing. But then there was this trouble about a supposed haunting, and so they changed their minds. Yet they were embarrassed or even mortified at what they were doing, so they kept it a secret. The only people who might have known about it would have been the girls' father and presumably their brother, who would have inherited the house next. He might have been quite keen to keep it quiet from his heirs in case it made them uncertain about inheriting this place themselves."

"People could be quite superstitious back in the eighteenth century. Supposing that the then Dunbar was concerned that if the heads were ever removed again misfortune would befall his family, and he didn't like to think to himself that one of his descendants would do such a thing?" Bainbridge concurred. "I think it is reasonable to assume that the family legend was kept quite quiet and that your great grandfather had no knowledge of the sisters."

"Then your aunt came along, found the old journals and spoke to people who had parents or grandparents who had served in this house," Victoria added. "She was prepared to go out and speak to people who your great grandfather would not have talked to, and she was the sort of person who would not be satisfied until she had solved the mystery. I think it is clear that she did not know about the skull in the attic."

"Why do you say that?" Dunbar asked.

"Because if she did, she would not have pulled up the drawing room floor and searched for the skulls there," Victoria stated "Maybe she learned about Oliver Cromwell's skull being up in this attic at a later date, but then you would have thought she would have realised that it was connected to the sisters and would surely have done something about it. I think it far more likely she knew nothing about the box."

"Then why did she insist I keep everything in the attic exactly as it was?" Dunbar remarked.

Bainbridge had been mulling this over for a few minutes and a new idea sprang to mind.

"What if we got this all wrong?" He said. "What if your aunt's injunction was nothing to do with the knowledge of a skull up here in the attic, but had everything to do with the fact that she wanted to make sure you didn't part with any of the old family belongings. She might have been concerned that you, as a new member of the family coming in and looking at everything with fresh eyes, might have been prepared to get rid of all this, and she saw it as much your heritage as the house itself. Equally, she realised the history contained in all these various boxes. What if it was an innocent arrangement? Nothing to do with skulls, but just to do with the fact she wanted to make sure the stuff in the attic remained where it was."

"Then I went and found the skull, and I made-up this story in my head that it was all connected," Dunbar suddenly realised how unnecessarily far he had gone in his conspiracy theories. "Maybe I have been looking at this wrong all along. After all, the skulls weren't even stolen by someone who wished me ill."

"It may be there is no connection at all to your family solicitor, and your cousin's attempts to claim this house for himself," Bainbridge agreed with him. "We have been seeing trouble where there is none."

Dunbar visibly relaxed at this news. His head sank against his chest.

"I cannot tell you how great a relief it is to hear someone say that," he sighed. "All these troubles I have imagined have been far worse than the reality. I really have overestimated all this."

"Try not to be so harsh on yourself," Victoria told him sympathetically. "We all came to a similar conclusion."

"Sir, apologies for interrupting this debate, but while we have determined how one skull ended up here in the attic, how do we explain how the second skull ended up in a coffin in the family vault?"

"It would appear that the skulls were not buried together beneath the drawing room floor," Bainbridge replied. "I am imagining there wasn't that much space between the boards and it was easier to bury them separately. One was disturbed at a later date by Mr Dunbar's great grandfather, but someone else must have discovered the other one at some point, and decided to move it to the family vault."

"We may never know for sure who that was," Victoria

acknowledged. "Though it would seem to me that it would be someone who knew who the sisters were, maybe someone who was close to them at the time. That is why they wanted them to be buried in the family vault."

"An idea has just crossed my mind," Bainbridge said, tapping his chin. "We are looking at things in a peculiar way. We are looking at them with a nineteenth century mentality when we should be looking at them with an eighteenth century mentality."

"What can you mean?" Victoria asked.

"In the early eighteenth century a suicide could not be buried in a graveyard," Bainbridge explained. "They could not be placed in consecrated ground. If it was known beyond the family that Eliza killed herself then it means she was never buried in the graveyard."

"But I thought my aunt spotted the gravestones," Dunbar said. "I thought they matched up with the dates that the sisters died."

"We assumed that meant that both sisters were buried in that graveyard. But let me give another suggestion. Supposing there is one gravestone, and upon it is written here lie the remains of Alice Dunbar, and also written on it is something like 'also in memory of Eliza Dunbar' and then it states when they both died. That does not mean Eliza is actually in the ground."

"You mean Eliza was buried somewhere else? Somewhere outside the graveyard? And one of her family members was so distressed by this, that they dug her up and removed her head and then buried it in the family vault," Victoria tried to get her head around this notion.

"Well, if you are prepared to dig up a head and place it beneath the drawing room floor to stop ghostly activity, would you not also be prepared to do something similar in regards to Eliza's head and place it in the family vault?" Bainbridge suggested. "We only actually know that Alice asked to be buried in the house, we assumed Eliza felt the same way. Maybe, someone just wished to have a part of her resting with the rest of the family. I cannot say for sure that is what happened, but it strikes me as a very reasonable idea. Where the rest of Eliza went we will probably never know."

"Why not bury all of her in the family vault?" Dunbar remarked.

"That is simple. There was a lack of space," Bainbridge held up his hands as if it was obvious. "You would never get two bodies in those coffins."

"It does make sense," Dunbar agreed.

"We have found answers for a lot of things this afternoon," Victoria nodded. "But we have not found the final clue we needed. There is no letter that tells us who killed Alice."

"May I suggest we all reconvene downstairs for supper?" Jennings said thoughtfully. "Once we are restored, we could spend the evening debating this further, but for the time being I think we all could do with a rest."

The butler had included himself with them as they now seem to be united in their efforts. Bainbridge and Victoria had to agree it was a good idea. They were tired and dusty. It would be good to have some time away from the stifling attic.

"We know a little more, at least," Bainbridge agreed. "And dinner shall surely make it all seem much more reasonable and logical."

Victoria gave a small huff.

"Dinner always does for you," she said wryly.

Chapter
Twenty-Four

V ictoria brought the engagement ring to the table when they
sat down for dinner. Something about it had caught her eye.
She found herself looking at it rather than concentrating on the food
before her. Her uncle watched her steadily.

"What is on your mind?" He asked her.

Victoria was toying with some vegetables at the side of her plate.
As was the habit for most family cooks, the vegetables were overdone,
boiled within an inch of their lives. No one seemed to appreciate raw
vegetables, or at least properly cooked vegetables, as Victoria did. Even
Mrs Huggins, Bainbridge's housekeeper, struggled with her unusual
diet.

Bainbridge watched her for a few moments, waiting for a response.
When none came, he politely coughed. Mr Dunbar looked up, but
Victoria didn't.

"Vicky?" Bainbridge asked, calling across the table.

Victoria at last lifted up her head.

"Did you say something?" She glanced across the table at him.

"What has got you so fascinated with that ring?" Bainbridge asked.

Mr Dunbar was now taking interest as well.

"Where did the ring come from?" He asked, having not been present when the ring was discovered.

"I found it in a trunk of belongings that seem to have been those of Eliza Dunbar," Victoria explained. "I found what appeared to be her wedding dress, and there were books that she had filled with notes and poems. I brought the books down with me as well, but it is the ring that caught my eye. A ring like this had to have been bought from a jeweller, and jewellers are very renowned for keeping long records. If this jeweller still exists, then perhaps they have a record of who bought this ring, and that will then tell us who Eliza's secret lover was."

"That is a very good idea," Bainbridge said.

"You do not need to sound so surprised," Victoria scolded him. "I am getting rather good at this detective business."

"I am delighted that I am rubbing off on you," Bainbridge beamed back at her. "I meant what I said. It is a good idea. I hadn't thought of it personally."

"Is there something in the box to tell you who the jeweller was that made that ring?" Dunbar asked.

Victoria turned the box over and looked at it for a bit. Then she glanced inside. She had to admit, in all the time she'd been studying it, she had not noticed any name of a jeweller. Often a jeweller's name was stamped onto the soft inner lining of the box. A logo or marking would indicate where it had come from. When that failed, sometimes it was on the bottom of the box. But in this instance there seemed to be no sign of who had made this ring or where it had been bought from.

"Curious," Bainbridge said, when Victoria had explained this anomaly. "Have you tried pulling out the lining to see if there is anything underneath?"

Victoria tried this and found that the lining was firmly stuck in place, she shook her head.

"I think it is just a dead end."

"Perhaps not," Dunbar said. "May I take a look at the ring?"

Victoria handed the ring to him and he turned it over in his hands.

"Are you thinking about maker's marks?" Bainbridge asked him.

"I am," Dunbar said. "If I can find a suitable magnifying glass, I shall be able to see if this is a maker's mark on the bottom of the setting for the jewel. Then we can compare it with known maker's marks and determine who produced this."

"We don't have a list of maker's marks," Victoria pointed out.

"Ah, but we do," Dunbar smiled. "You see, one of the things you don't know about my family is that they were rather fond of their gold and silver. Upstairs, in one of the rooms, there is quite the collection of jewellery, all locked in cases. And there is a book of maker's marks up in the library. In fact, there are several. All we need to do is compare this ring and its symbols to the marks in the book and see if we have a match."

Dunbar rose and rang the bell. In a short time, Jennings appeared.

"Jennings, do you know if we have in the house one of those special glasses that jewellers use?"

Jennings gave his master a strange look.

"I do believe that your late grandfather had such an eyepiece," he nodded. "Would you care for me to fetch it?"

"Yes, Jennings, and a book of maker's marks from the library, one that would hold those marks from the eighteenth century."

Jennings gave another nod and departed without a word.

"If this works," Victoria said, hardly daring to consider it, "we will know exactly who was behind the death of Alice."

"Knowing it, and proving it, will be two different matters,"

Bainbridge observed. "But maybe the person who wants the information does not mind if proof is limited. Maybe it will be enough for them just to know the truth."

Dunbar was pacing about his dining room, the ring still in his hand. He held it up to the window, and the sunlight glinted on the diamond.

"I thought the family legend said that Eliza's lover was poor."

"It said he was below the station of the family," Bainbridge replied. "Which is different to being poor. He may have still had money, but perhaps he did not have a title? Noble families could be very precious about titles. They still can be, for that matter."

"That is true," Dunbar nodded his head. "I am very intrigued by all this. I wasn't happy with the skull being in my house, of course, but now I am learning who it might relate to, I am finding it all somewhat more..."

He paused as he considered what the right word was.

"Interesting?" Victoria offered.

"Meaningful?" Bainbridge suggested.

"I was going to say entertaining," Dunbar frowned at them. "Is that the wrong thing to say?"

"I do not say it is wrong," Bainbridge smiled at him. "Perhaps not what we expected."

"Maybe after all, Mr Dunbar, you do have some of that family curiosity in you, that your aunt and your grandfather had," Victoria said.

Dunbar liked this idea. He smiled to himself as he thought about it for a while. It appealed to him to suppose that he wasn't so far removed from his family as he had thought, that he had inherited some of their fondness for mysteries.

"Maybe I will become a collector after all," he said. "Not of skulls, though. No, no, no. Never skulls."

"In that regard, I am relieved to hear it," Bainbridge told him. "For there are not that many skulls legitimately going about, and I would be slightly concerned if they all started to end up in your house."

Jennings reappeared with the eyeglass. It was a tubular device that fitted into one eye socket so a person could peer through it while holding the object in their hands. The late Mr Dunbar had used it when sorting through his geological finds.

Dunbar popped it into his eye socket and peered through the glass. He soon found it wasn't as easy to use as he had anticipated, and he fumbled with the ring, nearly dropping it, as he tried to work out what he was seeing. Victoria and Bainbridge waited for him to get the hand of it, mildly impatient.

"I think I see an H and maybe an A," Dunbar said at last. "I am not sure, however. They might be interlaced, and there might be an oak leaf or is that a K?"

Victoria tried not to sigh. Bainbridge merely rested his chin on his hand and waited for the unfortunate Mr Dunbar to try and figure out what he was actually seeing. There was a polite cough behind him, and everybody turned to Jennings the butler.

"May I look, Sir? In the past, your grandfather often asked me to confirm his findings on his stones. He found as he aged, his eyesight was not as good, and so he taught me the art of looking through the eyeglass to help him catalogue his finds."

Dunbar handed over the eyeglass. He seemed quite happy to do so. He had realised his own limitations. He gave Victoria and Bainbridge a weak grin, sheepish that he had not been as useful as he had hoped.

Jennings studied the ring for a while, carefully moving it about in the light so he could get just the right angle on the letters.

"I would concur with the identification of an H," he said. "But I believe the second letter is a stylised R. They are surrounded by a square which appears to have dots at each corner, very specifically placed as if they are part of the mark."

Bainbridge grabbed up the book on maker's marks before Victoria could. She glowered at him. He ignored her and fumbled through the pages, hastily coming across the section listed under H. There he traced his finger down the page, looking at all the different marks.

"Here we go. The mark you are looking at is from the firm of Humphrey Robsart, which were active in this county for quite some generations."

"I wonder if they still exist," Dunbar spoke. "That's the next problem we have to solve."

"Does this house happen to keep a street directory?" Victoria asked him.

Dunbar shook his head.

"Not to my knowledge. We have never really needed it, being out in the sticks."

"Then the only way to really be sure if this jewellers still exists, and if this is their mark, would be to write to the Gold and Silversmith Guild. They will be able to tell us if Humphrey Robsart Jewellers is still in existence, and if they are, we should be able to find out more about this ring."

Dunbar was glad of the idea.

"It sounds promising," he said.

"I shall begin composing the letter at once," Bainbridge told him. "We have at least something to be going forward with. We also have the books that Victoria found in the trunk. We should see if they have any clues to what was going on as well."

"What if we all retreat to one of the drawing rooms and go through one each?" Dunbar suggested. "We should use the very drawing room where the sisters were supposed to have had their heads buried. I rather think that would be a nice place to connect with them and maybe some spiritual presence might come to us and we will be able to find the clue we need."

Dunbar said no more, grabbed up a book and left the room. Victoria glanced at her uncle.

"Did he really just say spiritual presence?"

Bainbridge raised an eyebrow at her.

"At least he's not in a terrible dither about the fact there might be skulls beneath his floorboards or ghosts. That is something."

Chapter Twenty-Five

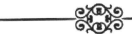

Bainbridge composed his letter to the local Gold and Silversmith Guild in Norwich and had it sent off immediately. With any luck, it would reach Norwich before the day was out. In the meantime, he wanted to spend a while reading the will he had discovered in the library. It was dated and signed and had been witnessed by two members of the staff. It had been authored by a gentleman named Peter Dunbar. Looking back through the family tree, Bainbridge determined that he was Mr Dunbar's great grandfather.

Bainbridge was curious why this particular will was not in the safe keeping of the family solicitor, and instead had been on the shelves of the library. He spent some time reading the conditions of the will and slowly gathered a picture of its somewhat surprising contents. It turned out that the Dunbar family had far more secrets than had ever been revealed.

The most intriguing of these secrets was that Peter had nearly completely excluded his eldest grandson, Mr Dunbar's cousin's father, from his will.

The family tree went as follows; there was Peter Dunbar, who had a son and a daughter. The son was named William, and he was the grandfather of the current Mr Dunbar. William had then had two sons of his own. The eldest was known as Jonathan and the youngest, Mr Dunbar's father, was known as Peter, in memory of *his* grandfather.

Peter Dunbar, senior, had excluded Jonathan Dunbar from his will. He had stated that Jonathan was to never inherit the house, nor any of his heirs. Yet there was something curious about this story, because quite clearly the will's clauses were not being upheld. Mr Dunbar's cousin believed he was fully capable of inheriting the house.

Bainbridge pondered over this for a while. In particular, he was curious as to why Peter Dunbar had wanted to exclude his eldest grandson from inheriting the property. It seemed a curious arrangement when most people preferred inheritance to go through the eldest male side of the family. It also explained, to a degree, why the house had gone to William Dunbar's daughter, and then, why she had willed it to the current Mr Dunbar. There seemed to be something in the background of all this that had not been explained to them.

The will was not explicit about the extenuating circumstances of this disinheritance, and Bainbridge was still concerned that this will was not in the family solicitor's keeping. It's presence in the house troubled him. Such a document should not be retained in the family property, but should be under safe keeping where it could be looked at by any future generations.

He decided that this was something he would have to investigate further when the time came. For the moment, however, he was more inclined to get back to the matter of Alice and Eliza.

He headed down to the drawing room, where Mr Dunbar was already sitting with Jennings in attendance. Victoria was not far behind them. She settled on a chair near Mr Dunbar and picked up one of the journals they had found in the trunk. Bainbridge joined them after being offered a cup of tea by Jennings.

"The letter is all sent and hopefully we shall have some answers soon," Bainbridge told them.

"That is good to hear," Victoria responded. "I do hope we can resolve this matter swiftly. I really feel for Eliza and Alice and their strange story. It must have been so sad for the sisters and I especially feel for Eliza who deemed it necessary to take matters into her own hands."

"That was certainly tragic," Bainbridge nodded. "Have you determined anything as yet from the notebooks?"

Dunbar glanced up from his reading.

"I have spent a lot of time going through this particular notebook. The girls went to all these dances, and the names in these books are fascinating. Why, they danced with the son of a lord, and another time they danced with soldiers from the local militia. It all sounds very romantic."

"Everything does when it's in the past," Victoria told him. "It's the nature of things."

"Well, I like to suppose that until the tragic events of Alice's demise, my distant relatives were having a great time of things," Dunbar said cheerfully.

"As yet you have no indication of who the illicit lover might have been?" Bainbridge asked him.

"Not so far. There are a lot of names. It could have been any of them. Eliza kept record of every dance she ever attended and, I have to say, she was quite sociable."

"Do any of the names appear familiar?" Bainbridge asked. "Perhaps we might see a particular connection to another local family?"

"In that regard, I am somewhat stumped," Dunbar admitted. "I don't know all the local names as yet. Don't forget I grew up far away from here. I have seen a couple that I recognise, but nothing particularly exciting. Intriguingly, the girls were friends with a Miss Haggerton who must have been a relation of the family solicitors."

"You did mention that they have been your family solicitors for a long time," Victoria agreed.

"And this most certainly proves it," Dunbar nodded.

Bainbridge picked up one of the notebooks near him. He glanced at the initial page and saw that it was dated 1729, the year that the sisters died. This intrigued him enough to start reading. He found similar lists in the book as Dunbar had already mentioned. Eliza liked to keep track of her dancing partners. She kept a detailed list, not just of who she had danced with, but how well they had performed, and to what music they had danced. Other notes included a list of the spring flowers she had spotted in the garden one day, or a recipe that she had come across, or the price of lace, and calculations to work out how much a new bonnet might cost her, or whether it would be cheaper to just retrim an old one.

It was a glimpse into a young girl's life and, certainly on the surface, it looked as though Eliza had had a delightful time. She had gone to dances, worn new dresses, met new people. She had enjoyed singing, drawing, spending time in the garden. There were so many social engagements, it was a wonder she kept up with them all, and yet, over and over again, there was no glimpse of the man she had intended to marry. Just who was he? And what did it mean that she had felt the need to hide the fact that he had murdered her sister? She must have loved him dearly, yet at the same time she had felt torn in her loyalties, which was why she ended up killing herself. She could not resolve her guilt over her sister's death with her loyalty to her secret lover. What a twisted web we weave, Bainbridge thought to himself.

"I think I have something," Victoria said suddenly.

Dunbar and Bainbridge both glanced in her direction, anticipating some good news.

"In this particular notebook, Eliza mentions a secret place she and her sister used to go to in the garden. They actually built it for themselves using old bricks from a wing of the house that had to be pulled down."

"That would have been the early Tudor wing," Dunbar said in a knowledgeable fashion. "I remember my aunt telling me about it, because there are some remains still in the garden. It was one of the original parts of the house, but it suffered badly in a storm and the chimney fell down, creating a huge gap in the roof, it was decided that the whole thing ought to be demolished rather than try and save it."

Victoria politely nodded at this irrelevant information Dunbar had recited so proudly.

"In any case, the sisters built themselves a sort of grotto with these bricks. It wasn't big, we are talking enough room for a doll to fit inside it. A child's thing really, like a doll house. However, as they got older, the sisters started to use it as a hiding place. They would place notes inside it for each other, and other important things they wanted to hide."

"It says all this in the notebook?" Bainbridge asked.

"Something along those lines," Victoria said. "Eliza writes that she went to the grotto to put in dance cards she wanted to keep hidden. I am not sure why she wanted to keep the cards a secret, maybe she danced with someone she ought not to have done, although there is no mention of any assignation afterwards. In any case, she would hide things in this secret grotto she did not feel it was safe to keep in her room. I am under the impression that the girls' mother, on occasion, searched through their rooms to see what they were up to, which is why the notebooks are so secretive."

"How does that help us?" Dunbar asked.

Bainbridge sighed at his inability to see how this would work in their favour.

"It means that the girls had a secret hiding place for important things, and perhaps that is where the letter Alice wrote revealing her killer has been placed. Of course, if it has been outside all these years, the odds of it surviving are very slim. On the other hand, it's always worth a shot."

"Where on earth would we begin to look?" Dunbar said thoughtfully. "The grounds are vast."

"If I may," Jennings interrupted. "I believe it would be prudent to speak to the gardeners. They will know of any brick grottoes in the flower beds or amongst the trees."

"They did not know about the family vault," Dunbar pointed out.

"No, Sir, but in that regard the woods are out of their domain. They do not garden in there, after all, but I would imagine the sisters did not build their grotto somewhere so secluded. More likely, it was relatively close to the house. Do not forget they had to carry the bricks there."

"I would suggest the likelihood is it is relatively near to where the old wing fell down," Bainbridge concurred. "Young girls are not going to traipse too far with a cartload of bricks to build a grotto. For that matter, they wouldn't be allowed to. We ought to take a look, and Jennings, I agree you should ask the gardeners if they have seen anything that could be considered a grotto."

"I shall do so at once, Sir," Jennings promised, and then he departed from the drawing room.

"This is all rather exciting," Dunbar said. "I have never taken much of an interest in the old Tudor wing, now it seems I should have. My aunt was very fond of it. She loved to show me the old remains. I'll take you there at once."

He jumped up, ready to set off. Victoria carefully put down the notebook she was working on.

"Well discovered," her uncle said to her. "You took two different pieces of information and found a common link. That is true detective work."

Victoria smiled. For once, this was a genuine compliment.

Chapter Twenty-Six

The remains of the Tudor wing were located to the west of the house. The Tudor wing had formed the original foundation of the house; it had consisted of a long hall in the traditional medieval style with an upper solar and some back rooms for the servants. It had been old fashioned even at the time it had been built. It had also been rather poorly constructed. Several hundred years of good winters had seen it tumble down and all that remained now was a grassy selection of lumps and bumps that indicated where once there had been walls and doorways.

Mr Dunbar took them on a tour around the old remains.

"My aunt liked to tell lots of stories about the Tudor wing. She always had a fondness for that period in history."

Victoria carefully negotiated her way over a lump in the ground which could have been some sort of wall. She tried to imagine when this had been an actual house, picturing a large room with a fireplace the family could gather around. She was usually quite good at imagining things, but in this instance she found it challenging to come up with a notion of what it must have been like.

"Obviously this whole place has been reduced to rubble for many years," Dunbar added.

Jennings had emerged from the side of the house and he gave them a nod.

"I fancy your butler wishes us to follow him," Bainbridge declared.

Dunbar glanced up and saw that Jennings was wandering towards another section of the garden.

"With any luck he has interviewed the gardeners and now knows where the grotto is," Dunbar said hopefully.

Jennings was walking towards where the old walls of the grounds delineated a neglected kitchen garden. There was an old archway where a gate had once stood. Jennings walked beneath it, with the others following.

Jennings headed for one corner of the old kitchen gardens and waited for them. There appeared to be nothing there at first, but when they came closer they realised he was standing in front of a box-like brick structure. It could have been anything and, at first glance, it did not immediately seem to be a grotto.

"The gardeners advised me to come and look at this," Jennings told them. "They all know about it, but no one has ever touched it. They are not sure what it contains, but they thought it was some sort of old fashioned beehive."

Victoria could see why they had thought it a beehive. The bricks were only loosely stacked together, with finger width gaps between them, similar to a beehive, though she very much doubted a queen bee would ever choose to nest in such a structure. It was too low to the ground for a start.

"Could this be the place?" Jennings said.

Bainbridge moved forward and carefully examined the brick box.

"In honesty, it does not remind me of a grotto," he said. "I actually recall many years ago that I had something similar in one of my gardens. It was designed as a meat larder."

"Why would anyone keep meat outside?" Victoria asked.

"It was designed to contain game which needs to sit around for a bit before people consider it suitable for eating," Bainbridge explained. "Some among the nobility prefer it if their game has gone a bit green before they actually receive it on a plate. The outside brick larder was supposed to be ideal for this, though I hear tell it did not catch on. Personally, I never used it. I prefer my meat to be fresh."

"On that front, we both agree," Victoria told him.

Dunbar was now crouched down in front of the brick box. He was poking at it with his finger, trying to see between the gaps.

"Shall we dismantle it?" He asked them.

"It is in your garden and therefore it is up to you whether it is dismantled or not," Bainbridge told him.

Dunbar only had to consider for a moment before he determined what he wanted to do. He picked up a corner brick and placed it to one side. This revealed very little. He then removed another brick along the same side. Bainbridge was peering over his shoulder.

"Be careful which next one you move. I think that they all interlink. If you move the wrong one, you could have the whole thing tumbling down."

As he said this, Dunbar moved the wrong brick and some others tumbled inwards. Bainbridge cringed, but it seemed that nothing had been damaged. Dunbar continued to remove the bricks, taking more care this time. Slowly, he revealed an inner chamber.

"Is there anything inside?" Victoria asked keenly.

All Dunbar could see for the moment was a dark hole. He started to remove further bricks so they could get some light into the interior.

"Maybe it *is* a meat larder," Bainbridge said.

Jennings stood to one side and remained silent. As further bricks were removed, and the space opened up, it became clear that this was not a meat larder. There was, in fact, a small box situated inside the construction. Hidden boxes seemed to have been quite a thing among the Dunbar family. Victoria stared at it with unease.

"Well, it is at least too small to contain a skull," she remarked.

Mr Dunbar carefully took out the box which was made of tin and had once been very prettily decorated. The decoration had chipped off over the many years it had been outside. Frosts and rain had stripped away much of the paint that remained and left it looking a sorry thing. There were a few streaks of pale pink and white left, with a hint of gold in places. It would have been a cherished item long ago, something to keep jewels in, or maybe face powder.

Dunbar held it tentatively.

"I almost feel nervous opening it," he said to them. "What if it contains nothing more than some childhood treasures?"

"We shall never know unless you open it," Victoria pointed out.

Dunbar still looked uncertain. After a moment of indecision, he fiddled with the lock on the box. It was only a basic latch that slipped over a nub of metal to keep the lid in place. It was rusted solid and his initial attempts to open it did not succeed. He tried rubbing at the nub with his coat sleeve. All this earned him was a dirty cuff.

"If I may?" Jennings politely interrupted.

"If you think you can do better, Jennings, by all means try," Dunbar said, handing over the box to his butler.

Jennings took the box with great care. He had a delicate manner of functioning, nothing ever seemed to take too much effort out of him. There was always grace and consideration to his movements. With that same diligent care, he tried the latch again, prising at it gingerly with a finger. It did not seem to move. He reached into his pocket and produced a small penknife. This he carefully edged around the latch trying to strip away the rust. When he felt that he had removed sufficient rust, he tried the latch again with his finger.

This time the latch moved upwards. It got stuck halfway, but with a little more jiggling it finally moved into a position which enabled him to open the lid. Once he had the lid open, it was clear to see that the contents had suffered from the damp as much as the exterior. There was something that looked a bit like paper inside; it had been folded over and was stained dreadfully from the water that had managed to seep in around the edge of the tin lid. If it was the incriminating letter they were hoping to find, it did not look promising that it had survived.

"I think it would be best if we took that back inside and opened it indoors," Bainbridge declared. "Having prior experience dealing with water damaged documents, I know it is advisable to have a cloth handy and some tweezers to help tease out the paper."

"I will bow to your greater knowledge, Sir," Jennings said.

They took the box and its contents indoors.

Chapter Twenty-Seven

The old dining room quickly became a scene like something out of a surgical operation. Bainbridge had Jennings lay an old sheet out on the table. Then he asked for a bowl with warm water, a soft cloth and a pair of tweezers. With great care he used the tweezers to take the folded slip of paper out of the box and placed it on the clean cloth.

"I say, that was my aunt's favourite tablecloth," Dunbar remarked, watching the procedure.

"If I may say, Sir," Jennings interrupted. "It was only her favourite because it was her prized cloth for displaying her finds on. She always cleaned her geological samples on this cloth."

"Oh," said Mr Dunbar. "That does make me feel better, Jennings, thank you. Carry on Bainbridge."

The old butler gave him a wise look, perhaps indicating that he would never put a tablecloth on the table if he thought it was his former employer's favourite for dining, and that he was slightly hurt Mr Dunbar had suggested he would be so careless. Dunbar, as always, was oblivious to his butler's thoughts.

Bainbridge very carefully used the tweezers to start to prise apart the letter. It had stuck to itself, and was covered with rusty dirt. Damp had sealed some of the edges together, and there was a hint of mould in places. Wherever the paper was particularly encrusted with dirt, and seemed to have stuck solidly together, he used a damp cloth pressed lightly on the paper to try to ease the pieces apart. The application of such a small amount of additional water caused the pages to become gently unstuck.

The operation took considerable patience and time. Bainbridge moved in a thoughtful manner, planning out each procedure as if it really was a surgical operation to save someone's life. In some regard, it could be viewed as something along those lines, except they weren't saving a life, they were rather redeeming it.

There was a clock sitting on the mantlepiece, Victoria found herself listening for the gentle ticking of the hands as the time passed. She was surprised how nerve wracking she found the whole procedure. It was, after all, just a piece of paper. Yet the more she sat there and waited for the unfolding to reveal what was within, the more strained she felt.

Jennings was watching quite intently. He seemed intrigued by Bainbridge's technique.

"Ever done anything like this, Jennings?" Bainbridge asked him.

"I confess, it is new to me," the butler replied. "I have never had to pull apart a dirty letter before."

Victoria felt a smirk cross her lips; there was something about the sentence that had sounded slightly rude.

"Have you done this before?" Dunbar asked Bainbridge.

"Once or twice," Bainbridge admitted. "Never before have I had a letter quite this old and in such a sorry state."

His eyes had never lifted from the paper. He focused now on gently teasing out the corners. Everyone was holding their breath. The slightest false move and a crease could rip, or a whole section of paper could disintegrate and they would never know what the contents were. As it was, it was hard to say whether the finished article would be readable.

"About a decade ago, I went to a mummy unwrapping," Bainbridge commented as he was working, speaking quietly was helping him to concentrate. "The mummy in question was some sort of priest. I recall how the gentleman in charge of the operation very carefully pulled back the ancient bindings. There was a real risk the whole thing would crumble to pieces. It was remarkable, all told, just what he achieved."

"I recall my aunt was very disparaging about the unwrapping of mummies," Dunbar added. "She fancied it was all wrong and that you destroyed more than you gained."

"She was probably correct," Bainbridge replied. "Though I have to say it is better to have them unwrapped and at least scientifically analysed, than to see them simply used as fertiliser or cast into train furnaces to be used as fuel."

"It is truly tragic what they do to these mummies," Dunbar replied. "My aunt intended to write a paper about it, but like so many ideas she had, it never came to fruition. She was always so busy with this, that and the other. She had more great notions than would ever be able to be completed in one lifetime."

"I think I would have rather liked your Aunt," Victoria said. "She sounds like quite a remarkable woman who knew her own mind, and was prepared to do anything to forward her ideas, even in a man's world."

"She was very much that. Even though I only knew her in her golden years when she had mellowed, there was still that flicker of determination and fire in her eyes. I admired her. She seemed to have such a focus for the way things needed to be. Something I cannot attest to myself."

Bainbridge nearly had the whole letter unfolded. He had teased out the fragile paper, which was like tissue after so long out in the elements. The edges were all stained a deep brown and water had seeped across a portion and made it hard to read the words, but he was relieved to see that the majority of the page was legible, even if the ink had faded to a pale ochre shade.

"I think a magnifying glass would be of great assistance," he mentioned to Jennings.

The butler immediately went away to find one, returning within a short span of time. Bainbridge took it and, with great care, leaned over the paper, examining it closely.

"Oh my," he said.

"Is it the letter the late Alice Dunbar wrote?" Dunbar leaned forward over the letter. He almost dropped his sleeve onto it, and Bainbridge shuffled him back quickly with a wave of his hand.

"This is indeed the letter Alice wrote," Bainbridge concurred. "It speaks quite plainly of the tragedy that befell her. She wrote quite clearly, considering how poorly she was at the end. This is her signature right at the bottom, still readable. I think the only sign that she was dying is the slight tremble as she writes which has caused the shakiness of some of the letters."

"What does she say?" Victoria asked, almost breathless at the enormity of it all.

Here they had a signed document telling them about the murder of a person. A murder that had been covered up for all these generations. It made her almost feel queasy with trepidation.

"Alice plainly states she is aware that her time is limited, and she wishes everyone to know what became of her, and how she met her end. I think it is plain to say she was most concerned about her sister, Eliza, marrying a man who was clearly violent. She does not mention justice or wanting to feel revenge for her own condition. She just wants to know that Eliza will be safe."

"The poor woman," Dunbar said sorrowfully.

"She explains how the accident occurred. She had confronted the secret lover of her sister. He had been in the house for some reason that she does not explain. They had met on the landing, and they had argued. She told him that she did not feel he was right for her sister, and that he should call the whole thing off. When he refused, she informed him she was going to tell their parents. The argument became more heated, and then he grabbed her by the arms and shook her. In the process, she stumbled, and her foot went off the stairs. She tumbled all the way down.

"Perhaps the worst cruelty of it all was the cad did not summon anyone to her aid. Instead, he fled the scene, having to walk past her to do so, and then left her to be found by someone else. I think it is safe to say that she does not paint Eliza's secret lover in an attractive light.

"After the event, she told Eliza what had occurred, but no one else. She wanted Eliza to know so that she could make up her own mind. But it was plain to her that Eliza could not condemn the man she loved. In desperation, Alice wrote this letter. I do not suppose we shall ever know how Eliza came to know of it. Perhaps she was with Alice when she died and happened to go through her belongings first before anyone else. Whatever the case, she discovered that Alice had written down who had killed her."

"You are torturing us with anticipation," Dunbar complained to Bainbridge. "Please sir, speak plain who did this?"

"There is a name written here," Bainbridge explained. "The writing is very faded, but it seems clear enough. Whether we can believe it or not, I suppose depends on our outlook."

"Julius, you are becoming trying," Victoria complained.

"Very well, I shall say the name, and you shall be surprised yourselves," Bainbridge nodded to them. "Alice writes that the man who killed her is named Mr Isaac Haggerton."

Bainbridge was right. The revelation did cause them to all hesitate. Dunbar, in particular, looked confused.

"Isaac Haggerton," he said, repeating the name. "You mean the man who became our family solicitor?"

Chapter Twenty-Eight

Dunbar looked quite confused. The revelation seemed less improbable to Victoria. It made sense that someone close to the family would be Eliza's secret lover, it had to be someone she met on a regular basis. She also recalled that in Eliza's diary she had kept a note of meeting with friends, including one known as Miss Haggerton. Was it so unlikely that this Miss Haggerton was the sister of Isaac Haggerton?

"This is quite a serious accusation," Bainbridge said to them all.

"You are quite sure of the name?" Dunbar asked feeling anxious that the family solicitor who had caused him such trouble might now be related to the murderer of one of his ancestors. The thought of saying this aloud worried him deeply. It could easily backfire on him and result in him losing the house.

"I am sure," Bainbridge said firmly. "I have looked at the name over and over and I am convinced it reads as Isaac Haggerton. I would stand up in a court of law and say as much, but if you would care to have another expert look upon it..."

"That will not be necessary," Dunbar said hastily. "I trust you, Bainbridge, completely. My concern is how on earth we could talk about this with Mr Haggerton. After all, it's his ancestor we're discussing, and he is a person who knows all about legal machinations. If I get this wrong, it could be very serious for me."

"I fear Mr Dunbar is quite correct," Victoria added. "A name in a letter is not much to go on. It is not exactly hearsay, but certainly not something that you could rely on in a court of law."

"I suppose everything depends on where we wish to go next with this matter," Bainbridge spoke. "If we merely wanted an answer, well, we now have it. If we want to actually make this public and claim justice for your ancestor, Alice, then we shall need considerable more proof than a name in a letter."

"Such as the proof that might come from knowing who had commissioned the ring that was given to Eliza?" Jennings said, then he turned and glanced to the clock on the mantel. "Sir, the letter should have been delivered by now."

"Then we should have news tomorrow," Dunbar understood. "I suggest we leave this mystery for the morrow. We shall lock away this letter in the safe in the study."

They all agreed this was the best plan for the time being. They each were exhausted by their investigations, and an evening to reflect on matters sounded exactly what they needed.

The letter was carefully placed on a cloth that was folded around it, and then it was secured in Mr Dunbar's safe. Victoria was somewhat reluctant to let it out of her sight, but decided she was being ridiculous. After all, she had not done very well with the dining room key when it had been in her possession. There was still the question of who must have taken it. A mystery she would like resolved before their time at the house was up. It had to have been the same person who was curious about the skulls' origins and had passed them the note. But just who was that person?

Despite Dunbar's wise suggestion that they take some time that evening to recuperate, she found that she was running over the problem in her head continuously. She could not let it rest; the thought that someone among the staff must be responsible nagged at her. Though she told herself to forget about it, it was on her mind all the way through dinner, and continued to plague her as she went up to bed that night. She fell into a difficult sleep and awoke once or twice with the same thoughts stirring in her mind.

Bainbridge, meanwhile, slept deeply and soundly. He had long ago learned that worrying about things in the early hours was simply impractical. It deprived him of sleep and thus made it harder to resolve a mystery the following day. Bainbridge believed that a detective owed it to his clients to be both well slept and well fed. It was the only way to solve a case.

Therefore, when they both rose the next morning, Bainbridge was as fresh as a daisy, while Victoria was crabby and weary. At breakfast, Bainbridge was the first to spy Jennings bringing in the morning's post. Jennings saw his meaningful glance and nodded to him.

"Unfortunately, Sir, among this pile there is no letter from the Gold and Silversmith's Guild. I took the liberty of checking the envelopes before I brought them in."

Mr Dunbar groaned and looked disappointed.

"There is a lot of day to go as yet," Bainbridge told him cheerfully. "It may be that our letter was not looked at last night. I have every hope that we shall have an answer today."

After breakfast, they retired to separate areas of the house, each lost in their own thoughts. Dunbar said he needed to catch up with his own correspondence. Victoria was still muddling over the difficulty about which of the servants might be responsible for the stealing of the key and the skulls. Bainbridge wanted to return to the mysterious will that he had found.

He laid it out on a table in one of the side rooms that no one was using, and found the magnifying glass. He studied the document at length, determining that it appeared quite genuine and that the signature did not look to have been adjusted, nor did the date appear to have been changed. But if this will was genuine, he still had the problem of why it was in the house. Bainbridge smelled a rat. It seemed that at some point he would need to go and speak to Mr Haggerton, and see exactly what the solicitor and his family were about.

He debated the matter for a while, then determined that there was no time like the present. With no news on the ring, he might as well follow up on the will, and it might give them an alternative solution to Mr Dunbar's problems about his home.

Bainbridge asked their host if he could borrow a carriage and horse. He did not want to disturb Victoria, as he felt she could do with some rest, and she had her own investigations, in any case. Not to mention, he was unsure if he was going to be on a wild goose chase with this matter of the newly discovered will.

Dunbar was curious as to why he would want the carriage, but did not ask questions, assuming Bainbridge was pursuing the case as instructed and trusting him in that regard.

Bainbridge set off with Imp as his driver. The curious fellow was very good with horses, and he drove them along at a brisk pace. He also knew the quickest route to the offices of Mr Haggerton. When they arrived, his keen eyes watched Bainbridge with intense curiosity as the latter headed into the premises.

Bainbridge found the offices were located in an early Georgian building, probably the same offices where the Haggertons had founded their business several generations ago. Being in a rural community, there was not a great deal of work for the current Mr Haggerton, in fact, his primary client was the Dunbar family, and that had been the same for his forebears.

As a result of this lack of trade, Bainbridge was able to speak to Mr Haggerton at once.

The solicitor was an oily little fellow with an obsequious manner. Bainbridge distrusted him immediately, and he did not believe his opinion was influenced by the knowledge that Haggerton was conspiring to try to get Mr Dunbar out of the family home. The solicitor rose and gave him a polite, old-fashioned bow.

"How may I assist you today?" he asked.

Bainbridge had informed Mr Haggerton's secretary that he was an academic researching the history of the area and wanted to look at some old documents he thought might be in the solicitor's possession.

"I had hoped to be able to see some old wills you may have in your possession. They would date back to the last century."

"May I ask what your interest in these documents is?" Haggerton asked.

Bainbridge was prepared for this.

"I am researching the lineage of the Dunbar family, as they are the most significant individuals in this area. I did visit the current gentleman of that name, but I am afraid his knowledge of his family's history was extremely limited."

"I can imagine," Mr Haggerton said darkly and with a degree of disdain.

Bainbridge continued to play on the solicitor's disregard for Mr Dunbar.

"I am having trouble tying up the family tree when it comes to certain outlying branches of the family. Mr Dunbar was reluctant to let me into his home to see if there were any papers that might assist me. That is when I thought I should come to you. As you are aware, wills often contain key information about family members, offering an indirect way of determining names, ages and their relation to the writer of the will."

"I see your point," Haggerton nodded.

"Would you consider allowing me to see the wills of past generations of the Dunbars? Seeing as they are no longer relevant to today?"

Bainbridge put on his most persuasive airs. Haggerton was thoughtful for only a moment. He liked the idea of getting one over Mr Dunbar, and going against his wishes for having this stranger look into the family tree. He agreed at once and escorted Bainbridge to a spare room where he could peacefully peruse every will in the possession of the solicitors.

Bainbridge was soon absorbed in his work, but there was truly only one will he cared for (though the others provided a fascinating distraction into the family arrangements of the Dunbars). It was not long before the will Bainbridge had been hoping to find lay before him. He read the words of Peter Dunbar and found this will differed in two significant details to the will he had found in the house.

First, Peter Dunbar had not disinherited his eldest grandson Jonathan.

Second, and certainly more troubling, this will was dated prior to the one Bainbridge had found in the house.

Chapter Twenty-Nine

B ainbridge was feeling deeply concerned as he headed back to Dunbar's house. The discovery of a second will suggested that some skulduggery had happened in the past. As far as he could tell, the will he had found in the house was perfectly legitimate. It had been witnessed and signed, and there was the name of the solicitor upon it. To his mind, someone had concealed the second will that was made at a later date to prevent the eldest grandson of Peter Dunbar being disinherited.

If that were the case, it implied it was someone within the family or, at the very least, it had something to do with the Haggertons. The more he investigated, the more it seemed that the solicitors and the family they represented had an insidious relationship. It was hard to say which side the true trouble was upon. Who had made the decision to mask the will? Was it a solicitor who was friendly to the family and wanted to ensure that the eldest grandson did not lose out on his inheritance? Or was it that grandson himself?

Whatever had happened, someone in the past had taken that

will, slipped it onto a shelf and assumed it would never be found. Considering the disorder of those shelves, and that all those particular papers had never been touched, they probably had a fair point. The problem was that Bainbridge had no information as to who the culprit had been. It would be easy to cast blame upon Jonathan Dunbar, who was the one who missed out on the inheritance, but he could easily be maligning an innocent man. He had the distinct feeling that trying to delve into this mystery was going to result only in disappointment. It was all too long ago. The witnesses were all long dead, and there was no one around who could reveal to him what had really occurred.

Mulling all this over kept him occupied as Imp transported him back to Dunbar's house. When he arrived, he discovered that Victoria had a similar look on her face as to the one he was wearing. He surmised that she had received similar bad news to him.

"Dare I ask?" He said, glancing in her direction.

"We have received a letter back regarding our enquiry about the jewellers who made the ring," Victoria said. "The maker's mark belonged to an old Norwich goldsmith. Sadly, they have been out of business for at least the last one hundred years and no one knows if there are any records left. We have yet again come to a dead end. We cannot prove that Alice was killed by Isaac Haggerton."

"We cannot prove it for certain," Bainbridge concurred with her. "But that does not mean we should give up. After all, we do now know some part of the truth and while we cannot prove anything in a legal sense, we can at least put to rest the minds of everyone in the household. We now know who those skulls belonged to, and what became of them. Justice may elude us, at least in this world, but, depending on your mindset, Isaac Haggerton has probably already come to his own justice in the next."

"That feels like cold comfort," Victoria replied. "I do not know where I stand on spiritual justice. I would have liked Alice's story to have been told in full so that everyone knew what happened."

"Everyone does know the majority of her story; that someone pushed her and she was fatally injured, and that someone was the mysterious lover of her sister Eliza. I also suspect that at the time of the occurrence, someone knew about Isaac and Eliza's relationship. Probably a servant, come to think of it, as they tend to know the secrets of the family better than the family themselves."

It was as Bainbridge said this that a thought struck him.

"Why don't we all go downstairs to the servants' quarters and have a chat with everyone? If you can gather together Jennings and Dunbar, we will all be together and I can propose something to you all."

"What do you know that I do not?" Victoria raised an eyebrow at him.

"You will soon discover that," Bainbridge told her. "Just do as I ask, and quickly."

It was not long before they were all downstairs and gathered together. The servants were all present and looked on edge. The last meeting they had had with Bainbridge there had been talk of people being dismissed, so it was not surprising that they seemed uneasy.

"I apologise for the seeming subterfuge," Bainbridge began. "It is not my intention to cause you anymore concern. I shall get to the point straight away. I have been out this morning to the offices of Mr Haggerton, and I have come across some information of significance. It does not immediately relate to the skulls we found, though I can confirm that we do now know the full story about those as well. Which matter would you like me to relate first?"

Bainbridge directed his inquiry at the servants. This intrigued them, they were not used to people asking them what they wanted. It was Mrs Moss who gingerly spoke up.

"Could you please tell us what you know about the skulls?"

Bainbridge nodded to her.

"I shall tell you everything I know. The skulls belonged to Eliza and Alice Dunbar. Back in the 1700s, Eliza was secretly engaged to a gentleman named Isaac Haggerton. Considering the name, and the fact the family did not approve of the match, I suggest this Haggerton was part of the dynasty of solicitors who have served the Dunbar family through the decades.

"Alice discovered that her sister had made this match and she was concerned. We might at first assume she shared the family's prejudices about such a union. But upon reflection, I believe her concern had much more to do with her love for her sister. I believe she considered Isaac to be a disagreeable man. She did not like his temperament and thought that he could be unpleasant. We can see from the actions that occurred later that she was right in her assessment. We have found a letter that describes the final fatal accident. Alice wrote it on her death bed, and she describes how she argued with Isaac about her sister, and that he pushed her down the stairs after shaking her. He then raced past her and abandoned her to her fate, determined not to be on the scene and to be associated with the crime.

"Despite his clear lack of a conscience, it seems that Eliza could not quite give up her lover to face the justice system of the day, and so she covered up the crime. We know the superstitious story about the girls' skulls. How Alice requested that her skull be buried beneath the new dining room floor, and that when that was not immediately done, a supposed haunting began. We need not go into that matter deeply, because that is another story all of its own. I don't deal in the supernatural myself, I leave that up to mediums and priests.

"I believe the reason Eliza's skull ended up in the family vault was simply because someone felt sorry she could not be buried in consecrated ground. She had killed herself, and could not be buried with the rest of the family. Someone decided that needed to be rectified, and they dug her up, took her head and placed it in the family vault, where at least she would be with other Dunbars. I doubt we shall ever know who did that unless we come across some more documents in the family archives and someone wrote down a confession.

"That brings us back to the matter of Isaac Haggerton. We have discovered very little about him and his association with the sisters. Aside from the letter that Alice wrote, all we have is an engagement ring that was among Eliza's belongings. It must have caused the family some curiosity when they discovered the ring after she passed. They would surely have wondered who had given it to her, but with no further details, they could not link it to a specific person.

"Unfortunately, we find ourselves in the same position. Though we now know that Alice gave the identity of her killer as Isaac Haggerton, we cannot substantiate the claim. The ring has taken us no further as we cannot determine who purchased it. We shall not be able to seek further justice for either sister, though I would like to think that we have resolved something in the mind of the person who was most concerned about these skulls.

"I have surmised that that person has long had connections to the family. Connections that went beyond the current generations of Dunbars. That stemmed back to a time when the sisters were alive. One of their ancestors must have been a servant here at the house and knew the full story. That person was only seeking redemption and justice for Eliza and Alice when they took the skulls and presented them in the way they were. It was perhaps a crass way of doing things, but it did get our attention."

"Yet it has not achieve what we hoped," Jennings interjected. "We cannot claim justice for Alice. We cannot speak of this more widely."

"That is true," Bainbridge agreed. "But I like to think that we have achieved enough, enough to put someone's mind at rest. We know the true story, and I shall ensure that it is written down and preserved in the family archives, so that it shall never be forgotten what happened to Alice."

"I am just relieved that this whole affair had nothing to do with someone wanting to get me out of this house," Mr Dunbar groaned. "The last few days I have lived under the dread of the thought that my cousin is determined to oust me from this property."

"In that regard, I have happier news," Bainbridge said, looking more cheery. "I believe, Mr Dunbar, that I can, once and for all, put your mind at rest. Your cousin cannot remove you from this house."

"What can you mean?" Dunbar asked trying not to look too eager.

"I have found a will amongst the family papers. It appears that someone hid it years ago. This will postdates the will that was originally read out as the authentic last testament of Peter Dunbar, your great grandfather. I believe it is the true will that he left behind. Someone hid it because in it, he disinherits his eldest grandson, Jonathan."

"Wait, my cousin's grandfather?" Dunbar asked, his curiosity excited.

"The very same," Bainbridge agreed. "Your great grandfather made it very clear that he did not want Jonathan Dunbar, or any of his descendants, to inherit this house. I have yet to find the reason for this disinheritance, and we may never know the true cause of the discord between them. However, what I can state is that Peter's will was hidden away, which indicates that someone wanted to pretend the disinheritance never occurred, but were not quite prepared to destroy the second will."

"Or someone saved it from being destroyed and hid it so that in the future it would be discovered," Victoria suggested.

"That is possible also," Bainbridge agreed with her. "Whatever the case, we now have it in our hands, and it is quite plain what it states. Mr Dunbar, you have nothing to worry about. Your cousin can never legally obtain this house."

Dunbar was stunned. Never had he supposed, when he had invited Bainbridge to his house, that such an outcome would occur.

"Why, that means I never have to deal with the horrible Haggerton man again," he said. "I can use a solicitor of my own choice. Bainbridge, you have taken a great cloud from over me. I was weighed down by this horrible burden, the fear that someone would take this home from me. Now at last I can rest easy."

"You can enjoy this home knowing you were always intended for it," Victoria smiled at him.

Mr Dunbar could only grin back. He gazed at the servants around him, wanting to rush up and hug them all, as if somehow they had been the magic that had created this triumph.

"Well, now," he continued, "can we go see Mr Haggerton at once and tell him the good news?"

Chapter Thirty

Mr Haggerton was surprised to see Bainbridge returning so soon. He was also curious, and slightly worried, that Bainbridge was accompanied by Mr Dunbar and a woman who had not been introduced to him. Mr Haggerton's last conversation with Mr Dunbar had not gone very well. It had been an unpleasant discourse where they had conversed about Mr Haggerton's views on Dunbar inheriting the house over his cousin. They had left on bad terms.

To see Mr Dunbar now looking positively chipper as he arrived troubled Haggerton deeply.

"Good morning, Colonel Bainbridge," he responded as cheerfully as he could manage.

He was suspicious that something was afoot and it wasn't going to be good for him.

"We are here about the will," Bainbridge told him, a smile on his own face.

"One of the wills you were examining earlier?" Haggerton asked uneasily.

"That is part of it, but I also wish to show you this will that I discovered recently in Mr Dunbar's home."

Bainbridge presented him with the will he had found among the papers in the family library. Mr Haggerton, if he had ever seen it before, showed no signs of it. He took the paper without hesitation and glanced over it.

"It is the last will and testament for Peter Dunbar," he remarked, staring at the paper. "I was unaware he kept his own copy of the will. What a pity, Colonel Bainbridge, that you were not able to just read this earlier rather than having to seek me out."

"You will note, Mr Haggerton, that this will was written after the will you have in your safekeeping."

Haggerton took a moment to peruse the will and spied the date at the bottom, he noted the signatures also.

"This appears to have been written several years after the will I have in my possession," he admitted.

"And would you say that this will is authentic?" Bainbridge asked him.

Mr Haggerton sensed a trap was closing around him, but at the same time he could not refuse his honest opinion. He was many things, but he was not a liar.

"From what I can tell of this paper, it is indeed genuine," he said. "The signatures are all in order, and I note that it appears to have been written by my own ancestor's good hand. In the past, the Haggerton's often wrote out wills for their clients themselves. It saved having to try and dictate all the legal terminology."

"Then this will, in your opinion, was written by one of the former Haggertons that looked after my family?" Dunbar said getting even more excited now.

Haggerton felt a familiar chill running down his spine. That trap was squeezing tighter.

"If you wished me to, I could compare this to the will I have in my keeping to see if the handwriting matches up, but I am pretty confident that this is the hand of one of my ancestors. I have seen his writing on so many documents it is easy enough to recognise, he has a certain swoop to his Fs and Ss."

"Very well, Haggerton, I am satisfied," Mr Dunbar declared. "Would you please read this will carefully?"

Haggerton glanced between the three newcomers, then he looked at the will. He was trying to think of a way to get out of this strange interview but there were no other clients that needed him. He, in fact, had very few. Most of his work was tied up with the Dunbar family. Pausing as long as he could before things became awkward, he cleared his throat, pulled out his glasses, and started to look through the will. The first part was unremarkable; it was largely legal terminology, the sort of thing you find in all wills, and it repeated much of what appeared in the will that he had in his possession. This consoled him slightly, and he read on with more enthusiasm. He was almost two thirds of the way through the will when he came across the segment that they had all wished him to see.

Now it was not difficult for him to hesitate. The colour drained from his skin as he read the words over and over. At first they wouldn't sink in, so he read them again. On his fourth repetition through the words, it finally dawned on him what they were saying.

"You will see that this is quite a complicated business," Bainbridge remarked.

"It changes everything," Dunbar said firmly, wanting to get to the heart of the matter quickly.

Haggerton cleared his throat again. It was a nervous habit. He glanced around, wishing there was something to drink at hand, anything that would give him a moment to compose his thoughts. In the end, all he could do was remove his glasses and place them carefully on the desk. Once this task was done, there was nothing else that could delay him in speaking the inevitable.

"Assuming that my assessment of this will is accurate and correct, it appears that there has been some error in the past," he said very carefully. "This will supersedes the will I have in my possession, and while nothing in particular changes as things stand, it does alter certain considerations we may have been thinking about in the future."

"You mean your plan to install my cousin in the house rather than me will come to nought," Dunbar said to him with a grin on his face. He was enjoying his moment of triumph.

"It seems there might have been some misunderstanding between us, Mr Dunbar," Haggerton said, smiling as best he could and trying to appease the man who now was the only thing between him and closing up shop. "I never intended to imply that I favoured your cousin over you. I have always fully supported your aunt's intention for you to be her heir. She was a woman with a sound mind and strong opinions. Who am I to deny what she wished?"

Dunbar almost wanted to laugh aloud at the sight of Haggerton squirming, and the way he changed his tune so quickly.

"You will obviously inform my cousin at once that he cannot make any claim against the house or the land," Dunbar said. "Naturally, we shall never know how the will ended up in the family archive instead of being with you as it rightfully should have been. We could suppose foul play, but perhaps it is better if we just imagine that there was a mistake in the past. Something quite innocent and innocuous."

"That would seem a reasonable assumption," Mr Haggerton said pulling at his necktie, which suddenly seemed to be cinching his throat in a constrictive fashion.

"It is pleasing to know that all this has been worked out for the best," Dunbar smiled. "I shall leave you in peace now, Mr Haggerton, you must have many letters to write to my cousin. He shall want a full explanation, of course. I believe I should take the will with me, however, as it seems to have survived so well in the family archive."

"It would be perfectly safe with me," Haggerton said, mildly offended at the implication that he might do something to destroy it.

"I am sure it would be, but if you don't mind, I would prefer it under my charge," Dunbar recovered the will from him and then he, Bainbridge, and Victoria headed out of the office, leaving Mr Haggerton trying to think how on earth he was going to explain all this to Dunbar's cousin, and how their plans to see him installed in the ancestral family home were at an end.

Victoria and Bainbridge spent the rest of the day tying up the few loose ends they had left. They made sure that the letter they had recovered from the hidden grotto was placed somewhere safe so that it could be preserved for the future. Maybe one day someone would find it, and understand what truly happened to Alice Dunbar, but for the time being very little could be done with it.

A quiet and private ceremony was held down at the now rediscovered family vault. Dunbar had asked the gardeners to clear around it so that it was once more revealed to everyone. Then they stood before it and said some appropriate words as the skulls were placed inside the coffin of Matthias Dunbar. Alice and Eliza were once more reunited in death. Mr Dunbar would arrange for brass plaques to be added onto the coffin lid with their names, so that no one in the future would wonder who the heads had belonged to.

It was very peaceful and seemed fitting. Afterwards, Dunbar remarked that at last he felt truly at ease in his home. He felt he finally belonged, as if he had been accepted by his ancestors after all this time. There was no longer a shadow lingering over him and he could enjoy his new home and the future he would have there.

Bainbridge and Victoria would spend one last night with Mr Dunbar, enjoying a thank you meal that he had specially arranged. Bainbridge decided to take one final stroll around the grounds before he left. He had fully recovered from his previous adventure and no longer felt as though he was gasping for breath. He had kept most of his concerns hidden from his niece, though it had crossed his mind that perhaps he ought to start taking short walks every day and improve his general fitness. It would do him no harm he determined.

He was just coming to the part of the garden where the Tudor ruins stood when he realised that someone was following him. He turned around and spied Imp. The strange little fellow gave him a nod and then sidled up towards him.

"I am off tomorrow," he told the colonel.

"Really?" Bainbridge said in surprise. "I thought this would be your home for the rest of your days."

"I only ever meant to be here a short time," he explained to him. "I came here for a purpose, but unfortunately things happened, and I wasn't able to complete my task until you came along."

"You have me at a loss," Bainbridge said, looking at him with a puzzled expression.

"Then I shall explain myself better. You see, my ancestor was once a servant to this family back in the 1720s. He was a groom here, and he was devoted to Alice Dunbar. When she died, he was considered a suspect though the family hushed things up and he went away. He never forgot Alice or what became of her, nor the shame that followed him for being suspected of the crime. He always wanted justice for her and for himself. The scandal meant he had to leave without references, and it was impossible for him to get another position as a groom. Things were very difficult for my family after that, and the bitterness it caused meant the story was passed down through the family all these generations."

"I can see why it left such a taint on your family memory. Then, you came here to clear your family name?"

"In a way, yes. That groom was my great, great, great grandfather. He lived a long time, well into his nineties, which was remarkable in itself. My great grandmother remembered him well and told my grandmother and mother how he seemed to be kept alive by wanting to right the wrong done against our family and Alice Dunbar.

"But nothing ever came of it. He died, still bitter at his failure. My mother told me the story as I grew up. We were very poor, and my mother made it plain to me that our poverty was a direct result of what happened to Alice Dunbar and the accusations against her great, great grandfather."

"Such a family legend can hold pretty powerful emotions," Bainbridge nodded his understanding. "It can leave lasting resentment."

"You have hit the nail on the head. As a young man I was filled with resentment. Life had dealt me a bad hand, that was how I felt, and all my anger was directed at the Dunbar family, who I had never met or even seen, but who became in my mind something of a monster. I did nothing about my rage, however, as I had my hands full just surviving. Then my mother grew ill and in her last days it became an obsession with her that our family had been cursed by the Dunbars to always be poor. She made me promise her, on her death bed, that I would right the wrong that was done against us."

Imp gave a shy smile as he explained this.

"That is how you ended up here, coming out of the blue with no one knowing who you were or why you turned up?"

"Precisely, Colonel, you see everything ever so plain. I told myself I was going to confront whoever was the head of the Dunbar family these days. I was going to give them a piece of my mind. I had so much hate inside me, I could almost imagine doing violence to them and not caring for the consequences. I believed they had ruined my family, led my mother to her early grave because they had cast us into poverty."

"An overwhelming burden to carry. Naturally you were filled with grief for your mother."

Imp nodded his head emphatically.

"There had only been me and her for as long as I could remember. I couldn't afford medicine for her in her last days. Maybe it would have done nothing, but I cannot help but wonder if I could have saved her if I had the money."

"And then you arrived here, and you met Miss Dunbar," Bainbridge elaborated. "What changed?"

"You never met Miss Dunbar, Colonel, so you cannot comprehend what she was like. She was goodness and kindness personified. I marched up to her door, a wretch in ragged clothes, full of fury, and she just smiled at me and asked if I would like tea and cake. She knocked the wind right out of my sails. She had Jennings get me food and clean clothes, then she asked if I had a particular reason for coming to her home.

"I couldn't speak the truth, not after how she had treated me. I mumbled something about needing work and there and then she gave me a job. Jennings was not impressed, but she would hear none of it. I told myself, if I took the work, I could quietly go about finding out the truth about Alice Dunbar's death, but I never did. I started to like it here. I started to really like Miss Dunbar and I did not want that to change. Then she died and I felt this terrible guilt that I had become so distracted and had forgotten about my poor old mother."

"Then you were the one who pickpocketed Victoria and stole both skulls."

"It was melodramatic, I know, but I needed to get your attention and I fancied if you thought there was some threat to Mr Dunbar you would pursue the matter harder. I never picked any pocket, by the way. I came in and out through the window. I never intended to risk coming through the house. I think you might find your niece has a hole in her pocket and the key fell out not long after she had locked the dining room door. One of the maids found a key on the floor and put it away in a drawer."

"And because no one was asking about a key, she did not mention it."

"Don't suppose she gave it a second thought," Imp shrugged.

"That explains it. And you wrote the note?"

"One of the maids helped me with it. She is not to get into trouble for all this, you appreciate she did not know what she was doing. She was upset after we were called into the drawing room and questioned. I barely persuaded her to say nothing about it."

"I fully understand," Bainbridge nodded. "And I think it's safe to say you did this family a service in the end."

"Thank you for understanding, Colonel. I knew you would," Imp grinned. "And thank you for helping my family, I hope now that my ancestor shall be able to rest in peace."

"There is one final question I have for you," Bainbridge said. "I am curious about your name."

A mischievous grin came onto Imp's face.

"There is no great mystery there," he chuckled. "My family have always had a peculiar fashion for names. My great, great, great grandfather, who was the groom here, was called Importance Smith. I was named after him, especially as my mother fancied I would have something very important to do in solving the family conundrum."

"And it easily shortened to Imp," Bainbridge joined in his amusement.

"Very easily and it suited me."

"Then I wish you well on your travels Importance."

Bainbridge held out his hand for Imp to shake. The man was quite taken aback by the gesture and shook the colonel's hand with both of his.

"Take good care of yourself, Colonel."

With that Imp hurried away, to disappear back to where he had once appeared from. He happened to pass Victoria, who was coming out to see where her uncle was.

"What a peculiar fellow," Bainbridge smiled as she approached.

Victoria gave him an odd look, not sure what he meant. Bainbridge nodded at her.

"I will explain later," he chuckled.

"Now all is concluded, we are to head back to Norwich?"

"We are indeed, though it is rather late in the day to leave now. I imagine Mr Dunbar would not begrudge us one final night here."

Victoria tried not to sigh. She was keen to get back to her own surroundings, safely away from mysterious skulls.

"By the way," Bainbridge added, "I think you may have a hole in your dress pocket."

Victoria fumbled to turn her pocket inside out and there discovered there was a large rent in its seam. She stared at it aghast.

"How did you know?" She asked her uncle.

"Ah, just another example of my miraculous detective abilities," Bainbridge preened.

Victoria glared at him, but nothing she did would cause him to tell her the truth.

"That is how you lost the key of course. It was never stolen," he added.

"Have you ever been told you can be quite unbearable?"

"Repeatedly. I take it as a compliment. Now, I fancy one last stroll around these gardens before we leave. Care to join me?"

He held out his arm to her. Victoria grumbled to herself but took his arm.

"Only to keep an eye on you," she said.

"Of course," Bainbridge smirked. "Someone has to."

They strolled off into the gardens, another mystery solved and Bainbridge feeling fully restored to his usual vigour. He just hoped they had managed to finally give peace to Alice and Eliza Dunbar and, if they were looking down upon their descendant, he hoped they would wish him well in his new venture.

Mr Dunbar was almost certainly going to need it.

Enjoyed this Book?

You can make a difference

As an independent writer reviews of my books are hugely important to help my work reach a wider audience. If you haven't already, I would love it if you could take five minutes to review this book on Amazon.

Thank you very much!

The Gentleman Detective Mysteries

Have you read them all?

The Mayfair Mystery

The fifth mystery

Murder on Ice

The sixth mystery

The Man of Friar's Wood

The seventh mystery

The Cherry Tree Murder

The eighth mystery

Also by Evelyn James

The Clara Fitzgerald Mysteries

Memories of the Dead

One murder. Two suspects. Bad things happen when you mess around with a mother's grief.

Clara Fitzgerald is struggling to make her name as a private detective in 1920s Brighton, when most people think women cannot solve crimes. Undaunted by the prejudice she faces, she sets out every day to her humble office in the hope someone will ask for her help.

Then she meets Mrs Wilton; a scatter-brained, emotional widow who believes her dead husband can lead her to lost treasure from beyond the grave. Ignoring her better judgement, Clara is drawn into the case. There is nothing she detests more than people abusing another's grief and that is exactly what a fake psychic is doing to Mrs Wilton.

Wanting to help and understanding Mrs Wilton's grief all too well, Clara makes a promise to aid her. But when matters take a dark twist, Clara finds herself accused of murder. Can she prove her innocence, along with proving herself as a detective?

Memories of the Dead is the first novel in this cosy, entertaining, historical murder mystery series by Evelyn James.

If you love engaging, quick-witted, no-nonsense female heroines solving dastardly, mind-boggling murders – and doing it all while armed with no more than a sharp hatpin or fire poker – then you'll love Evelyn James' page-turning, 1920s, detective series.

Available on Amazon

About the Author

Evelyn James (aka Sophie Jackson) began her writing career in 2003 working in traditional publishing before embracing the world of ebooks and self-publishing. She has written over 80 books, available on a variety of platforms, both fiction and non-fiction.

You can find out more about Sophie's various titles at her website **www.sophie-jackson.com** or connect through social media on Facebook **www.facebook.com/SophieJacksonAuthor** and if you fancy sending an email do so at **sophiejackson.author@gmail.com**